MY AUSTRALIAN STORY

A BANNER BOLD

The Diary of Rosa Aarons

Nadia Wheatley

A Scholastic Press book
from
Scholastic Australia

This book is for my god-daughters, Siobhan and Gabrielle.

LEXILE™ 980

Scholastic Press
345 Pacific Highway
Lindfield NSW 2070
An imprint of Scholastic Australia Pty Limited (ABN 11 000 614 577)
PO Box 579
Gosford NSW 2250
www.scholastic.com.au

Part of the Scholastic Group
Sydney • Auckland • New York • Toronto • London • Mexico City
• New Delhi • Hong Kong • Buenos Aires • Puerto Rico

First published in 2000.
This edition published in 2005.
Text copyright © Nadia Wheatley, 2000.
Cover copyright © Scholastic Australia, 2005.
Cover design by Antart, Sydney.

Reprinted in 2009.

National Library of Australia Cataloguing-in-Publication entry
Wheatley, Nadia, 1949–.
    A banner bold : the diary of Rosa Aarons,
    Ballarat Goldfield, 1854.
    For upper primary, lower secondary school children.
    ISBN 978-1-86504-852-9.
    1. Eureka Stockade (Ballarat, Vic.) – Juvenile fiction.
    2. Gold mines and mining – Victoria – Ballarat – Juvenile fiction.
    3. Ballarat (Vic.) – History – Juvenile fiction.
    I. Title. (Series : My Australian story)
A823.3

Typeset in Adobe Jenson.

Printed by Tien Wah Press, Singapore.

10 9 8 7 6 5 4 3 2   9 / 0 1 2 3

Ballarat Goldfield,
1854

In writing I hereby ask no favour from my reader.
A book must stand or fall by the truth contained in it.

Raffaello Carboni, *The Eureka Stockade*

Prologue

On The Queen of the South
The Ocean
Northern Hemisphere
The World
The Universe

15 April 1854

Meine liebe *Jennychen*,

    What a fluster everyone is in! There is a ship on the horizon, sailing homewards, and as the sea today is as calm as a bowl of soup (green soup! Maybe turtle . . . or horrid spinach) the Captain has said that we may send a boat across to it, with letters. On all the decks, everyone is scratching away with pens and pencils. Well—nearly everyone. My new friend Tom isn't (he cannot read or write), and neither is Mama, for she is sewing me a cool gingham dress to wear in the hot hot hot Antipodes.*

    So—what news do I have to tell you? Well, none, really, for nothing happens on a ship. (Unless, of course, you are fortunate enough to be shipwrecked, and cast upon a desert island, like the Swiss Family Robinson.

But that has not happened to us yet.)

Yes, although we are only a week at sea, already I am missing our plays and performances. I am writing a new one—Judith and Holofernes—about the Jewish heroine who saved her people from tyranny. I know you will love it, especially when Judith goes into the King's tent and plunges the dagger into Holofernes' stomach and he is so fat that it disappears completely, handle and all! And then she slashes off his head—she must have a second dagger, hidden in her sleeve—and the maid carries the trophy home, all bloody in her basket. And of course all the people cheer because Judith has rescued them. Then the curtain falls.

I can just see this working splendidly with you as the maid. I would be Judith of course, and we would have to use one of our fathers as the wicked King Holofernes. (Probably your father, because he is a lot fatter than mine.) Tom is a good companion (for a boy) but of course he would be no use at all as the maid. So without you, I am lonely.

I was complaining about that to Vati this morning. He was already starting his first report to your father, and he suggested that I write a sort of journal like a serial for you, and put it in the parcels he sends to the Mohr.

Yes! I thought. And I can send you a copy of the

play too, when it is finished. Perhaps you could be Judith, and Laura could be the maid. (Or Lenchen.) Of course, I will probably not be able to post anything more until we arrive at Melbourne. Or maybe I will wait until I reach Ballarat, and then I will send you a lot of pages together. I warn you—I will not be writing to you every day, Jennychen! Not unless something exciting happens. And besides, I have all my lessons (including of course my Word of the Day, which I have to choose).

But now I must stop, as Mama is calling me. The lesson I did not tell you about is Needlework. Yes, even on the boat, I have to do that! You know how much I abominate it.

Till next time—
Your friend, Rosa.

* 'Antipodes' is my Word for Today. Do you like it, Jennychen? In our Greek lesson this morning, Vati made me derive it. 'Anti' of course means opposite or against. And I worked out that the 'podes' bit had to mean 'foot' or 'feet'. But how could something be against feet? My father drew it like this:

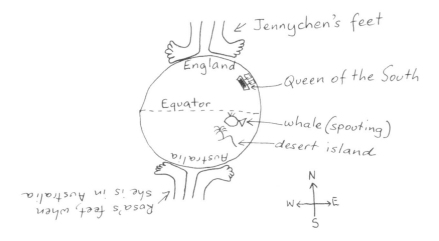

See? When I am in the Antipodes, my feet will be opposite to yours! I expect that when I am an Antipodean, everything will be upside down. I am so looking forward to it.

(Yes, Mama. I am coming! Wretched Needlework! I hope they don't have sewing in Upside Down Land.)

Journal

Monday 17 April 1854
On *The Queen of the South*

It seems there is a Very Important Person on our ship, Jennychen.

Some of the sailors allow Tom and me to help them polish the brass, and they have told us that Sir Charles Hotham is also bound for Melbourne on *The Queen of the South*. He is to become the new Governor of the new Colony of Victoria. A couple of the sailors spat and cursed as they said his name, for Sir Charles was formerly a Naval Captain, and has a reputation for being very harsh on his crew. (His nickname is 'Old Quarterdeck'.)

Still, I do not suppose it much matters what he is like, for we do not mix with the passengers on the top deck. (Mama and I are in a cabin with eight other ladies, and Vati is in one of the men's cabins. Of course we could not afford to have a cabin just for our family. Mama and the other ladies are seasick quite a lot.)

Friday 21 April 1854
Weather has been foul for four days. We cannot go on deck, the squalls are so bad. To pass the time, Vati and

I have begun to memorise 'The Rime of the Ancient Mariner'. We plan to know the whole poem by the time we reach Melbourne. My father is also reading me *Don Quixote*, and by myself I am reading *Peter Simple* by Captain Marryat. How I love that story! I have decided that if I am not a famous playwriter and actress when I grow up, I want to be a Post Captain on a man-of-war, just like Peter Simple. Of course, I would have to dress up as a boy. What a lark that would be!

Tuesday 25 April 1854

Nothing much to report. The wind has dropped so we have got steam up now (about 10 knots an hour, Vati says). Tom says he saw porpoises this morning, but I did not.

Vati and I are making great progress with the Ancient Mariner. We are up to the part where he is cursed, after shooting the albatross, and he sees the slimy things crawling with legs upon the slimy sea. It is such an easy poem to learn!

(Of course I still learn my ten lines of Shakespeare each week, and my ten lines of Goethe. And Vati has promised that when we are settled in our new home, he will start to teach me Latin. You can see that I am determined that I shall win our competition, Jennychen!)

waves

Monday 1 May 1854

We crossed over the Line last night shortly after 12 o'clock. I was asleep of course but Vati came and tapped on our cabin door and Mama and I went up on deck with him. There was nothing to *see*, and I was not standing upside down on the deck or anything, but it seemed especially special because of it being May Day (although I realise that the 1st of May cannot be the start of Summer, now that we are in the Antipodes). And it was exciting just to be up on deck at midnight.

The stars were far brighter than you could ever see them in London or Paris—but of course some of the stars are different too, because we are around the other side of the earth, looking up into a different part of the heavens! In particular, there is the most beautiful cluster of five stars, which Vati says is called the Southern Cross. Mama began to talk quietly in Yiddish to my father, about how she feels that we are coming at last to our Promised Land. Usually he becomes a little impatient when she talks like that, but last night he reached his arms around me and Mama, and held us both, and I felt so happy. The Southern Cross is going to be my special wishing sign, here in the Antipodes.

Although it is still very early and Mama and the other ladies are fast asleep, I have decided to go up on deck. I feel as if there is a whole new world to explore!

Later . . .

The oddest thing happened this morning! I was up on deck, by myself, when suddenly there appeared over the rail a strange man with long green seaweedy hair and a golden crown, and there was more seaweed draped over his green robes. You have guessed—it was King Neptune himself! He asked me my name, and where I was bound, and he wanted to know whether I had crossed his Dominions before.

Later, when everybody was up, he made his appearance again, accompanied this time by his bride and child, a doctor, a secretary, a barber, six policemen and four bears. As the band played *Rule Britannia*, they marched all around our deck, before progressing up to the top deck where only the rich passengers are allowed. (The bears of course were just sailors dressed up as bears, but I swear that Neptune was real.)

Sunday 14 May 1854

The last few days, we have been sailing. The sailors say that we are doing about 260 miles a day, and if we continue at this rate, we shall be in Melbourne before we know it!

Tom and I see plenty of Cape pigeons and albatrosses flying about. (We are near the latitude of the Cape now.) The pigeons are so pretty, but some of the gentlemen up on the top deck shoot them for sport. They make bets about the number they will hit. It is very cruel, because many are wounded, and are left to suffer. Sometimes the dying birds fall on our deck, and Vati scoops them up and drops them into the ocean, so that they may drown and die quickly.

Monday 15 May 1854

The most ghastly thing happened this morning, Jennychen. The gentlemen on the top deck were shooting pigeons again. Usually Mama and I sit down below in our cabin when that is happening, but this time we were on deck with Vati, and suddenly an albatross landed on the boards in front of us. It had been shot by mistake, and was bleeding all over the deck, and flapping its huge wings and making the most hideous cry.

I saw my father's face and it was full of dread, and I knew of course that he was thinking of the Ancient

Mariner. And yet he picked up that flapping bird and, turning his head so that he would not have to look at it, he wrung its neck to put it out of its pain. Then he gently carried it to the stern of the ship, and let it fall down into the ocean, where I watched it float upon the waves for a few moments before it finally disappeared.

It was only then that my father looked up to the top deck, to see what the gentlemen were doing. But the shooting had stopped, and they had all disappeared. Later, the sailors were whispering that it was Sir Charles Hotham himself who shot the bird. They are very superstitious about it, and fear that it will bring bad luck upon our voyage.

Mama is ill, and has had to go and lie down in the cabin. I know that she fears that it will be my father who catches the curse, and not the Governor.

Tuesday 6 June 1854

TROUBLE!

This morning Tom and I decided to have an adventure. Well—I suppose I decided. And Tom followed.

It was so early that no one was around—not even any of the sailors—and after so many weeks of walking up and down the lower deck, I felt like exploring. 'Come on,' I said to Tom, and I started to climb up the ladder.

'We can't go up there!' Tom warned me.

Passengers like us are not allowed to go up to the top deck, where the gentlemen and ladies might be strolling about.

ENTRY FORBIDDEN.

That is what the sign says. But how can they forbid me to climb up to where the wind blows?

I put another foot on the ladder. 'Don't worry,' I told Tom. 'We will just have a quick look, and come down again. No-one will see us. Promise.'

And so he followed. Up and up, until we reached the top deck. The air smelled so fresh there, I felt almost like one of the seagulls, wheeling high above us. But it wasn't only the cry of the seagulls that I could hear . . .

'*Someone's coming!*' I whispered to Tom.

Quick as a flash, we slipped into a tiny space behind a lifeboat.

It was still so early that when I heard the voices I thought it had to be a couple of my sailor friends, maybe polishing the brass or scrubbing the deck. I am not afraid of sailors.

But then—looking underneath the lifeboat—I saw three pairs of feet. And the instant I saw them, I knew that they did not belong to sailors, for these feet were inside soft leather boots, as shiny as new money. Above one set of boots I could see a pair of trousers made of fine blue cloth, and above another set of boots there was a pair of trousers made of cloth that was a pale yellow colour. The third pair of legs was wearing the white trousers of a soldier's uniform, and I could even see the tip of a sword hanging down.

And now I could hear voices coming from the other side of the lifeboat. The owners of the feet had decided to stop and have a conversation right in front of my hiding place!

'Of course it is vital that I establish my authority, right from the start,' a voice announced. It was coming from where Mr Blue Trousers was standing.

'Yes,' Mr Yellow Trousers agreed. 'You need to show them who is in charge.'

Yabber yabber yabber . . . 'Legislative Council,' the voices were saying, 'Fiduciary insolvency . . .' It was even more tedious than listening to Vati talking to your father, Jennychen, about Politics and Economics! And Tom and I were so squashed that my left leg had quite gone to sleep.

'Spare the rod and spoil the child,' Mr Blue Trousers went on. 'It is my belief that that maxim holds as true for a colony.'

Suddenly I found myself realising who Mr Blue Trousers had to be. But before I could actually remember his name, I saw the rat.

Mama says that I always exaggerate but I swear—

this particular rat had long hairy whiskers and beady red eyes, and it was as big as the foot of the new Governor of Victoria, who was so busy going *yabber yabber yabber* that he didn't even notice the rat running right between his two blue trousered legs . . .

And now it was scuttling under the lifeboat . . .

Straight towards Tom and me!

My own leg was so fast asleep underneath me that I could not have moved for all the gold in the Colony. Poor Tom didn't have the same trouble. As the rat ran onto his leg, he let out a scream—and tumbled out of our hiding place, onto the deck.

The next thing I knew, a hand was reaching in—a hand in a red coat decorated with gold braid—and I was dragged out by the soldier, who kept a tight hold of me with one hand and of Tom with the other.

The Governor of Victoria was looking down his long pointy nose at us, as if we were worse than the rat! And as I looked into the cold grey eyes of Old Quarterdeck, I found myself remembering the stories I had been told, about him keelhauling sailors, and sentencing them to a hundred lashes, and I truly thought for a moment that he was going to tell the soldier to throw us overboard—just like that! His face was so cruel and so mean. But suddenly he pursed his thin lips and said to the soldier: 'Just get rid of them,

Lieutenant!' Then he turned on his heel and strode off down the deck.

Mr Yellow Trousers waddled after him, like an obedient little puppy.

And now the Lieutenant was shaking us. '*Do you realise who that was?*' he kept asking as he dragged us back down to the bottom deck.

. . . Mama says that she is mortified. She means because she was ashamed in front of the other ladies, when I was brought down here like a convict. 'Why do you do these things?' she asked me

'I just wanted to feel free!' I told her.

Vati of course is not really angry, but he pretends to be. He says that I have to sit quiet and write my journal for the rest of the morning. And so that is what I am doing now. It is not really a punishment. As Vati knows. I can see him winking at me now, over *Don Quixote*. In a minute I will go and ask him what Sancho Panza is doing.

Wednesday 7 June 1854

And now I am in even worse trouble. The Lieutenant just came back, and he asked my father to come up to the top deck and speak with the Governor. Mama is pretending to sew, as if nothing is wrong, but I know she is worried. So am I . . .

Later

I am forgiven. Even by Mama.

Yesterday, when my father was apologising on my behalf to the Lieutenant, he mentioned what he does for a living. And when Sir Charles Hotham found out that Vati writes articles for the *Pall Mall Gazette* and the *New York Tribune*, he was keen to be interviewed about what he plans to do in Victoria.

Meine liebe Jennychen, you should have seen my father's face when he came back!

'*The man's a complete martinet!*' That's what Vati said to Mama.

I thought that sounded like a sort of long-legged bird—mainly white, with a flash of black on its wings, living in marshes, eating worms and slugs—but when I looked it up in the dictionary (because of course I decided it *had* to be my Word for the Day) I found it means a sort of tyrant.

Anyway, Governor Hotham plans to rule Victoria with an iron fist, my father says. 'He told me his first aim is to get rid of the Colony's debt.'

'And how does he plan to get the money?' my mother asked.

'By squeezing the miners,' Vati replied.

'That will make him popular on the goldfields!' Mama said. I knew she meant the opposite of course.

'I told him that,' Vati said, 'and do you know what he replied?' He read from the notes he had taken. '"I have complete confidence in my ability to maintain order and suppress riot at any cost." That's what he wants me to write in my articles. He wants to impress his masters back Home with how strict he plans to be.'

'And will you write what he wants?' Mama asked.

'Yes, of course I will,' Vati told her. 'But I will make my own comment about the likely outcome of such a policy.'

'Why?' I asked. 'What do you think will happen?'

'I think that if someone goes looking for trouble,' Vati said, 'then he is likely to find it.'

Well! I know Vati is writing an account of this meeting to your father now, so I have written it down for you as well. I still miss you and often feel lonely, especially as Tom's father has forbidden him to play with me any more. Poor Tom was also whipped. Sometimes I think that we are so lucky to have the fathers that we have.

Have finished the *Judith* play now, and am making a clean copy for you.

Wednesday 21 June 1854
Almost in Melbourne

We are here! Or nearly! Oh Jennychen, I am so excited. I am sitting on the deck writing this as we come through the heads. The little pilot boat has come out to shepherd us across this bumpy bit of sea called 'The Rip', and through the channel into Port Phillip Bay. All the passengers are up from the cabins, so it is very crowded. Vati has his arm around Mama, in case she gets squashed. Most of the travellers on this ship are on their way to the goldfields, so the men are cheering and some are calling out things to the shore like: *'I know you are waiting for me—my great big golden nugget. I'm coming, my darling!'* It's really funny. But they're all laughing and wishing each other *'Good luck!'* Tom's father even nodded to me—that's how nice people are being!

Oh, I am far too excited to write!

1 o'clock in the afternoon
Now we are about to anchor, near a place called Sandridge. There are so many ships here, the masts look like a forest. I can see quite a few buildings now, but it is nothing like coming up the Thames to London! Our guide book says that the sand in Victoria is as golden as the nuggets in the earth, but Sandridge beach looks grey and gritty, like Brighton. (I tell Vati that when he writes

his guide book, he has to write the TRUTH.) The weather is bleak and cold, with showers. So much for the hot hot hotness! Vati says today is the Winter Solstice. Imagine that! Everything really is upside down here. (We should be having Christmas pudding for dinner!)

In a couple of hours we ordinary passengers will be taken to the pier by a barge. However, my sailor friends have told me that the Governor has to stay on board until tomorrow, when a huge Procession is planned to welcome him. I am glad we are not so grand. I cannot wait to learn to walk upside down!

Later: At Mrs Wood's Private Board and Lodging House
Actually, you would have laughed, Jennychen, to see me step on shore, for I may as well have been upside down. After so many weeks at sea I found that my legs would not walk properly upon land. I wobbled and rolled, like a drunken sailor!

Luckily, Vati bought tickets on an omnibus, so we travelled the four or five miles into Melbourne town in style—in an open wagon pulled by two horses. The streets here are wide, but so muddy. And when we crossed the main river, even that was brown and muddy (as if it were upside down). Vati says it is called the Yarra Yarra. I suppose that must be the language of the Aboriginal people. I wonder if I could learn to speak it.

Then I would know German, French, English, Yiddish (a bit), Ancient Greek (a little), Latin (soon, when I learn it), and Australian. You would never be able to beat me then!

Anyway, it is evening now—our first night on Antipodean soil. Well, we are not actually on *soil*, but have squashed into a lodging house in Little Collins Street East. Mama and I are to share a cot in a sort of cupboard under the stairs, and Vati will sleep upstairs in a room with eight other men. Melbourne is so crowded with people going to the diggings that we were very lucky to find anywhere at all to stay. At the supper table this evening there were men from Poland, Mexico, France and Spain as well as from England and California. They are all on their way to the diggings. (There weren't any other children.)

Thursday 22 June 1854
Melbourne

Today is a Public Holiday. All the shops and businesses are shut, so that everyone can welcome the new Governor. Vati grumbles over breakfast—'Why should we take part in a Royalist circus?'

'A circus!' I start to get excited, thinking he means a real one. But Mama explains that he just means a lot of Silly Fuss and Bother.

Anyway, as he is unable to buy provisions or go about his business, he agrees that we may as well join the crowds that are going to line the route all the way back to Sandridge, where His Excellency will receive his formal Welcome. On Mrs Wood's advice, we decide to watch the cavalcade as it comes over Princes Bridge, across the upside down river.

Vati is smoking a pipe on the porch with some of his new friends—Monsieur du Maurier from France, and Señor Borges from Spain (who looks just like Sancho Panza!) and the funny man who comes from California. But now Mama is ready at last, so we are off! The day is bright and sunny, although still cold.

Later

What a spectacle, Jennychen! I swear, I have never seen a Procession so grand, nor a crowd so vast—not in London, nor Vienna, nor even Paris!

Luckily, we were on the Bridge early, so managed to obtain an excellent position, next to a parapet for me to stand on, and a little ledge for Mama to sit upon. Although we had a long wait, the crowd was so curious that I was never bored. (I even saw some Aborigines, with blankets as cloaks! I wished I could talk to them, but of course I do not know their language—except for 'Yarra Yarra'.) There were people selling lemonade and all manner of pastries and pies, and there were brass bands playing, and a man with a little monkey doing tricks. And from every window of every building there flew streamers and Union Jacks. (The Colony uses the British flag, because of course it does not have one of its own.)

Over the centre of Princes Bridge there was a huge Triumphal Arch made of leafy green branches and decorated with flags and mottoes, with a floral crown at the top and wooden carved figures representing an Emu and a Kangaroo. On each side of the arch was written, in blue letters on a white background:

VICTORIA WELCOMES
VICTORIA'S CHOICE

I thought it sounded pretty but Vati scribbled it into his notebook and muttered: 'That puts the situation in a nutshell.'

'What do you mean?' I asked.

My father explained that 'Victoria' is the name of the Queen as well as the name of the Colony—which of course I knew (sometimes Vati thinks I am a total ignoramus)—so if you translate the pun, it means that the Colony welcomes the Queen's choice of ruler.

'When will these people start to demand the right to elect their own rulers?' Vati asked. He looked around the crowd, as if this were Germany or France back in 1848, and any minute now the Revolution might begin.

It was midafternoon and my legs were getting tired when people began to say—*'They're coming! They're really coming at last!'*—and I climbed up onto my observation post and saw the Official Party of the Mayor and members of the Legislative Council, with Lady Hotham in an open coach and the Governor on horseback, escorted by the soldiers of the 40th Regiment, together with the Mounted Police. As they processed beneath the Triumphal Archway, the crowd was shouting 'WELCOME' and 'HURRAH' so loudly that it sounded like the roaring of the ocean. The band began to play, and everyone sang *God Save the Queen* and then *Rule Britannia*. (Everyone except of course my parents and me.)

After the military band there marched all sorts of groups and societies—carrying banners and wearing special costumes, and often led by their own band of musicians. I cannot tell you them all, Jennychen, but I remember there were the Welsh Colonists, the American Colonists, the German Colonists (I gave a special cheer), the Sons of Saint Patrick (led by a harpist in a pure white robe, with long grey locks and a flowing beard), various lodges of Freemasons (in their uniforms), the Licensed Victuallers, the Total Abstinence Society, the carpenters and builders, butchers (in blue frocks, white trousers and straw hats), and the farmers (wearing ears of wheat in their hats). The printers had a huge wagon, with a printing press on it, and there were men on the wagon dressed in Masonic orders and wearing the cap of Liberty, and they were printing off a history of the new Colony of Victoria from its birth, four years ago, right up until today! I thought that was special, but behind them— guess what there was?

I shouted into Vati's ear, 'Look! Look! Here's the Royalist circus!' Actually, it was called Mrs Rowe's American Circus. And it was just wonderful, Jennychen. There were eight of the most beautiful white horses, and on them were the performers, wearing cloaks of sky blue. I swear they were far more splendid than His Excellency! I begged Vati to let us go to the circus while we are in Melbourne. He has said, 'We will see.'

Last of all in the cavalcade there were hundreds of schoolchildren carrying leafy branches and Union Jacks, and singing. I wished I was there with them, being part of the Procession, instead of just watching. (Do you ever wonder what it would be like, to go to a school?)

Sunday 25 June
The Parlour, Mrs Wood's Lodging House

If I were Queen of Australia, I would ban Sunday afternoons. They are so tedious! At the moment Mama is resting, Vati is out on the porch talking with Señor Borges and Mr Jameson (the man from California), and in the parlour I am the only person who is awake.

We have spent most of the last two days SHOPPING! Buying all sorts of things that my parents think we will need in our new life. As you know, Vati does not actually intend to dig for gold, but will be collecting information for his newspaper articles and his guidebook. But even though we shall be living in a lodging house in Ballarat, my parents still bought lots of things like tin plates and pannikins and candles and writing paper and dried figs and sago and lanterns and lamp oil and oilskin coats and boot polish and flour and sugar and Edam cheese and potted anchovies. What with our portmanteaus, and the trunks that are still on the ship, I do not know how we will get it all there! 'Don't they have shops in Ballarat?' I asked, and Mama explained that they do, but people say that everything is very expensive at the diggings. Not that things are cheap, here in Melbourne. Would you believe that Mama was charged sixpence for a needle, and pins sell for as much as a penny each?

In between all the shopping, we have been sightseeing too. Melbourne is extremely small, but public buildings such as the Town Hall, Post Office, churches and so forth are built of stone and are quite grand. Our lodging house is close to the Treasury Gardens, where Mama likes to stroll. There are two Theatres—the Queen's and the Royal Victoria—but they do not seem to have plays, but rather advertise performances such as Fireworks and Ethiopian Comic Dances. Mrs Wood told Mama that the ladies who go there smoke short tobacco pipes in the boxes and dress circle. I should love to see that, but I could tell from Mama's face that we would not be going.

In Little Bourke Street many of the shops are owned by Chinese gentlemen with pigtails. We even went into a little shop, where scarlet and gold paper lanterns hung from the ceiling. After Vati bought some ink and Mama purchased some tea-leaves, the proprietor gave me a good luck charm to wear around my neck. He said it will help me prosper.

'Will I find gold?' I asked him. (I thought he said 'prospect'.)

But he gave me a mysterious smile and told me that riches come in many forms.

Yesterday morning, Vati went to see the Editor of the *Melbourne Herald*, to ask if they would like to take any articles that he might send from the diggings. After he left us, Mama took me back down Bourke Street. I thought she must want more sewing materials, because that is where the drapery and tailors' shops are. But yesterday they were all closed, although other shops were open.

'Why are they shut?' I asked Mama.

'Because it is the Sabbath,' she told me. Then she pointed out a small square building, set back from the road. 'That is the Melbourne Synagogue,' Mama added.

As you know, Jennychen, we do not follow the old customs, any more than your family does. But as we stood outside the gate, I saw that Mama's eyes were shut, and she was very quiet and still.

'What were you doing?' I dared to ask, as at last we walked on down the street.

'Giving thanks for our safe arrival. And asking that all goes well, in the future.'

That seemed like a good idea. And then Mama took me to a confectioner's shop. And that seemed an even better idea! I swear, the variety was as fine as you would see in Vienna, and I found myself unable to choose between two types of licorice, orange chips, candied lemon, crystallised banana, motto kisses, bonbons with conundrums . . .

It wasn't long after we arrived back at Mrs Wood's

that Vati appeared—very pleased with himself, and pleased with me as well. For as soon as he had brought out the interview with Governor Hotham, the Editor had bought it on the spot. 'My good fortune is all because of my naughty little daughter!' my father said.

I told him, 'That is my Prosperity from my Chinese charm that you are sharing.' And Mama of course couldn't stop smiling.

And now I can hear my father laughing outside on the porch with Mr Jameson. So I might go out and see what the joke is. (Mr Jameson knows a great many jokes. And he wears a silver belt buckle with gigantic bullock horns on it. Mrs Wood says all the Americans are very flash.)

Monday 26 June
Still in Melbourne!

This morning Vati went out to Sandridge to see when our trunks would be unloaded, so Mama and I set off down Swanston Street, to take a stroll in the Botanical Gardens.

In front of the Town Hall, we saw a number of people crowded around a man in a red shirt and a wide-awake hat. (That is what people call the wide-brimmed hats that the diggers wear.) From a distance, I thought he might be a juggler or a conjurer—but when Mama and I got close we saw that he was burning bank notes! Yes, he was lighting them, one after another, holding each one up, so that everyone could see it burst into flame. And do you know what he was complaining about? He was saying that he had brought nice clean *fresh* gold down from Ballarat, and the bank had given him dirty old notes in exchange. So he was burning his paper money, piece by piece.

'Plenty more where this comes from!' he started to shout, and Mama hurried me on. (I think he was drunk.)

Of course, not everyone in Melbourne is wealthy. On the south bank of the Yarra Yarra there is a canvas city made up of thousands of tents. Mrs Wood told us that these belong either to people wanting to go to the goldfields, or to others who have tried their luck, and failed to find gold, and have come back penniless.

She also told Mama that there are many children in this city who have no home, because their fathers have run away to the diggings, and their mothers are unable to feed them. It is unfair, that there should be such great wealth and such great poverty, side by side.

Bad news when we arrived back at Mrs Wood's. Our trunks are still on *The Queen of the South*. Vati says that many of the sailors have taken 'French leave' and have run away to the diggings, so there is no-one to unload the hold. We may be forced to stay in Melbourne for some time. My father is out on the porch now, talking about the problem with Mr Jameson and Señor Borges and Monsieur du Maurier.

I do not think this is a good moment to ask my parents about going to the circus.

Friday 30 June
On the Ballarat Road
Weather: wet, cold (despite a thick guernsey and my oilskin coat)

I am writing this in pencil as I sit on the dray, bumping along a rough dirt track. (Well, it is mud, actually.) Yes, Jennychen, we are on our way at last! Vati's new mates (that is what men call each other, in the Antipodes) helped him unload our luggage from the ship, and we have joined their expedition to the diggings. Mama and I are up on top of the trunks, while Vati walks ahead with Mr Jameson and Monsieur du Maurier. Sancho Panza is leading the horse that is pulling the dray. (Her name is Tulip, and she is a chestnut with a white blaze on her nose. As you know, I am a little afraid of horses. But I patted her this morning, and she made a friendly whiffling sound, as if she was saying, 'Hello, Rosa.')

My father as well as his friends have swags on their back. (A swag is an oilskin wrapped around a couple of blankets and some provisions for the road.) The three others also have large knives or tomahawks in their belts, and Mr Jameson carries a gun as well, in case we meet any Vandemonians. (They are former convicts, from Van Dieman's Land.) Mama says that by carrying a gun, he is putting us in more danger. But of course, we cannot object, because we couldn't get to Ballarat without Vati's new mates, and Mr Jameson is their leader. (He dug for gold in California and is the only one who knows what to do.)

Last night, one of the other lodgers drew a little map, to show us the way. First we are to head west, across the Keilor Plains. Then we will go through a place called Bacchus Marsh, and across the Werribee River. I cannot imagine what the marsh will be like, for already it is as if we are making our way across a giant bog hole. Ballarat is seventy-five miles from Melbourne.

Later (nearly sunset)
I have just seen a whole herd (flock?) of kangaroos, bounding across the track!!! Mr Jameson calls them 'boomers'.

Later still: camped beside the track
Too tired to write. Mama and I are to sleep under the dray, and Vati and his mates will sleep in the open. It is

raining even more heavily now. Vati is trying to light a fire, but all the wood is wet. I do not think he has ever lit a fire out of doors before.

Saturday 1 July
On the Ballarat Road (which is just mud mud mud mud mud mud mud mud MUD)
Weather: pouring rain

Mama and I walked all day today because the dray was too heavy for poor Tulip to pull through the mud, with us on top. We got bogged about a dozen times. My flannel petticoat is thick with mud. Mama and I will squash in among the trunks on the dray tonight, as it is too muddy for us to sleep on the ground.

Monday 3 July
On the Ballarat Road
Weather: sleet!

(We are stopped now for a little break.)

As we slog along the track, Vati and I are trying to find words for what we are walking through. So far we have got:

bog	marsh	fen
swamp	ooze	mire
slime	slush	slough

Alphonse (that is Monsieur du Maurier) has helped me remember a French word to add to the list: *la boue*.

(Did I tell you that Alphonse is twenty-two years old? He is the only digger I have seen who does not have a beard. And he wears a red-and-white striped hat like a nightcap. Mama likes him because they talk French together. She still does not much like speaking English.)

Tuesday 4 July
On the Ballarat Road
Weather: rain (clearing a little this evening)

Walked all day again. Tonight the men have made a huge bonfire because it is American Independence Day and J J* says we all have to celebrate the Glorious Revolution, when the American Colonies broke away from the British King and became a Republic. The Frenchman and J J are teasing the rest of us and asking when are we going to make Republics in England and Spain?

'We are not English!' Mama says crossly. 'We are German nationals.'

But of course, Germany is a Monarchy too.

'Perhaps we could make a Republic in Victoria,' I say, just to be funny.

But the adults nod their heads, as if I have said something that is obvious.

It is nice to be warm by the fire, and Mama is cooking potatoes in the ashes. J J is opening a bottle of what he calls 'nobbler'.

* That is what everyone calls Mr Jameson, because his name is James Jameson. Mama said it was rude for me to call a grown-up by a nickname, but J J won't let me call him 'Mister'. He says that no-one on the diggings gets called by his full name. The men all call me 'Rosie Posie'. It feels friendly, like being in a big family.

5 July, 1854
Beside the Melbourne Road, Ballarat!
Weather: rain in the morning but clear skies by afternoon

The sun is setting by the time we make our arrival. As we come up the Melbourne Road, we can see a host of little flickering lights, that Vati says are people's camp-fires. They make me think of the gold and scarlet lanterns hanging inside the darkness of the Chinese shop. It is too late to go into the Township, so once again we make our camp beside the road. At least tonight it is not raining. Sancho Panza makes a good fire, and Alphonse cooks fried steaks and boiled eggs, while J J teaches Mama to make a type of bread called 'damper', out of flour, water and baking soda. It is our first proper meal since we set off.

Afterwards the other three men sit around the campfire, drinking nobblers and talking about all the gold that they are going to find, but Vati sits with Mama and me, up against the dray, and we look out at our new home. I can smell smoke, but it smells so different from sour black coal smoke in the fire back in London or Berlin. Here it is a fresh *green* sort of smell that comes from the leaves of some of the trees that grow here. Vati tells me that people call them 'gums' (because of the sticky stuff that comes out of the trunks), but their botanical name is 'eucalyptus'. Then of course he cannot help but give me a lesson as we sit in the darkness.

'See if you can derive it,' he says.

I know the 'eu' bit means it is a Greek word.

'*Kalyptós*,' Vati says softly. '*Kalyptós* . . . Tonight I will be *kalyptós* by my blanket.'

Suddenly I know. 'Covered!'

'Yes,' Vati tells me. 'Before it opens, the little flower of the eucalyptus tree is covered by a leathery case, to protect it.'

'Like you wear boots,' Mama tells me, 'to protect your feet.'

A flower with boots! See what I mean about how strange this country is?

But Vati is going on with the Greek lesson. He has another 'eu' word for me. '*Eureka*,' he says. 'What does that mean?'

Easy! Everyone knows that that was what Mr Archimedes shouted when he got into his bath, and he discovered—well, he discovered something very important. 'I have found it!' I tell Vati.

'What?' Vati pretends not to understand. 'What did you lose?'

'Silly,' I say to him. 'That is what *Eureka* means: "I have found it".'

And Vati tells me that here in Ballarat *Eureka* is also the name of one of the areas of the diggings. It was called that a couple of years ago, when an especially rich vein of gold was found in an ancient dried up riverbed, deep under the ground.

'And from the map,' Vati says, 'I think that the Eureka area is probably just down the road a bit.'

'Is that where we'll live?' I ask.

Vati suddenly becomes silent.

'No,' Mama says. 'We will live in a lodging house, in the little Township.'

My father still does not say anything, so I tell him that I want to sleep in the open tonight. I do not want to be *under* the dray, or *in* the dray. I want to feel the upside down Australian soil beneath me, and watch the starry sky above. Mama shrugs at Vati, and so he puts down an oilcloth, and then a blanket, and makes a little nest for me.

And now I lie in my little blanket nest on the upside down earth, and I look up into the heavens and I see the Southern Cross . . . But I wonder—if the earth is upside down, then is the sky downside up?

I do not want to write any more because I want to let myself spin right down into the deep blue sky . . .

These are gumnuts.
They hold the little eucalyptus flowers.

Thursday 6 July 1854
Ballarat
Weather: fine! Still cold but not raining! Hurrah!!!

Dawn

The rain has stopped and everything should be wonderful, but I feel tired and out of sorts. I seem to remember this strange dream, in which my parents were arguing, and Mama was really angry, and telling my father that he *cannot* do something. It almost feels as if it were real. But it must just be a dream. For of course my parents sometimes disagree, as all parents do, but Mama would never never try to tell Vati what he can do and what he cannot do.

I must have fallen asleep again (if I was ever awake) for it is early morning, and here I am, writing to you, Jennychen, as I watch Vati gather more wood to boil up a kettle full of water that Sancho Panza has fetched from a stream. (I mean—a creek!)

Mama is hanging the blankets on a gum tree to dry, and her face is very angry and when my father asks her if she would like a cup of tea, she does not reply.

I wonder what is going on. I wish they would not fight, on our very first day in Ballarat. (I have learned that the name is Aboriginal for 'Resting Place'. It is now four months since we set off from England, so it feels good to find our Resting Place at last. It makes me think of Mama talking about our Promised Land.)

Afternoon

I have a new best friend! He is black and he is beautiful, and his name is Bonaparte. And I fell in love with him on first sight! I met him this morning, as Mama and I went for a stroll from our camp site, around the nearby diggings. (Vati did not come.)

Oh Jennychen, you would be amazed at the sight of the diggings. The whole area—as large as a London suburb—is like a gigantic ants' nest, with thousands of ants busily digging away at separate little holes. Except of course when you get closer you see that the ants are men, with bushy beards and red or blue shirts and moleskin trousers and wide-awake hats and handker-chiefs tied around their necks. And you have to imagine that the ants are very very noisy ants, for there is a constant banging of the cradles.

(No, the cradles are not for babies, Jennychen. That's what I first thought when J J talked of his cradle. But a goldmining cradle is like a wooden box on a rocker,

This is a goldmining cradle.

and the diggers wash the dirt in it, to see if there is gold among the clay.) Anyway, the noise of the cradles down by the creek is like ten thousand drums beating, all through the day. Keeping time with that rhythm, there is the cranking sound of the thousands of windlasses as the buckets of dirt are wound up from the mines.

But if the diggings are like an ants' nest, you also have to bring into your mind that picture of the tournament in your King Arthur book. You know the one I mean—with all the tents and the coloured pennants. For in between the ant mounds there are tents and tents and more tents (some with red tops), and from many of the tents there fly bright flags, and more flags fly above the ant mounds. At breakfast this morning J J explained that most digging parties have their own flag, and they fly it above their homes and workplaces so that people are able to find them.

'What is your flag going to be?' I asked him and Sancho Panza and Alphonse, for of course they are going to work as a team together.

'Perhaps you and your mama could make one for us, Rosie Posie,' J J suggested.

I thought that was a grand idea, but Mama just put her pannikin down on a log, gathered up her skirts and walked away. I do not think Mama likes the man from California.

It was soon after that that she told me that we would go for a walk. 'And leave the men to their business.' I wished that Vati would come with us, but he stayed with his mates around the fire.

Anyway, he will be sorry when he discovers what happened. (We are back at the camp site, but now Vati and the other men are away somewhere.) We met Signor Carboni! Do you remember him, Jennychen? My parents knew him in London a couple of years ago, so I expect that your family knew him too. He is very funny and kind, but the best thing about him is that he writes plays! In between trying to find gold, of course. He told Mama that he has been in Victoria for eighteen months, at other diggings as well as Ballarat.

'And what of your esteemed husband?' he asked my mother.

She sighed. 'I fear that he is developing an acute case of Yellow Fever.'

My heart stopped when I heard that, for I expect it is like Cholera or Typhoid Fever. Perhaps he caught it on the boat.

'It is very infectious . . .' Signor Carboni was shaking his head. 'And in some cases there is no cure.'

I could see Mama making those grown-up signals that mean 'Not in Front of Children', and so it was at that point that Signor Carboni gave a whistle—and the next thing I knew I was being kissed and licked by darling Bonaparte. (Oh, he is so adorable, Jennychen.)

Later, when I tried to ask my mother what is wrong with Vati, she went quiet once again. I am very worried. I hate the way grown-ups think that they shouldn't tell children bad news. Tonight on my wishing stars I am going to wish that my parents would be nice to each other. Or at least tell me what is happening.

It is nearly evening now, and the men still are not back. Mama is calling me to gather wood for the fire, so I must stop.

Friday 7 July
Ballarat

I dreamed last night that my father started turning yellow—first a sort of sallow colour, then the colour of butter, and then more yellow and more yellow. And then he suddenly just—disappeared.

Am too anxious to write any more.

Sunday 9 July
The Gravel Pits, Ballarat

For all the diggers, Sunday is a Day of Rest. So for the first time the beat of the cradles and windlasses has stopped. And even here at our camp site the frenzy of the last couple of days seems to be halted, and no one is shouting 'Rosa! Hold this rope!' or 'Fetch us the hammer, Rosie Posie!' or 'Come and hang out this washing, *meine liebchen!*' Now Mama is struggling to cook a leg of mutton in the camp oven, and the men are sitting on the logs around the fire, mending their boots or darning their socks or writing letters home (Sancho Panza has three little girls back in Spain), and Vati is writing up notes for his guidebook, and I can hear a bell being rung at the little Chapel that is on the edge of this field and the Eureka field, and for once even the million mad dogs of the diggings seem to be quiet. (Of course my darling Boney does not count as one of the mad ones. He came to visit us last night in our new home— along with his owner of course.)

Yes, Jennychen, we are settled at last in our very own little tent in our very own little camp site up the hill from our very own little goldmine!!!

Well—the mine isn't really ours, I suppose, because Queen Victoria owns everything underneath the tiptop surface of the Colony. But on Friday, Vati and J J and Sancho Panza and Alphonse each bought a licence to dig down and look for gold inside a little area about the size of our tent. They found this place on Thursday, and J J is certain it is going to be a real beauty. Vati couldn't stop talking about it when they came back to the camp that night. 'We're going to make our fortune!' he cried, and he picked me up and whirled me around and around.

'Look at you!' Mama told him. 'So much for your Socialist beliefs!' she said. 'You are as greedy as the next man! What will the Mohr say?'

My father did look a bit uncomfortable then, and I do wonder what your father will think when he learns that Vati has caught Yellow Fever. But Vati said that if he is to write good reports for the newspapers, and a good guidebook about Australia, then he really needs to experience everything first-hand.

Now that I know that Yellow Fever isn't going to make my father die, I do not mind if he is infected! And I would rather live in a tent on the Gravel Pits than in a lodging house up in the Township of Ballarat. There are a lot of children living around here—and even more on the Eureka field, where all the Irish people live. Already I have met a girl called Sal, who lives nearby. (Well, her name is really Salvation, but she said to call her Sal. She has the longest, thickest, blondest plait you have ever seen.)

Of course, now that Vati will be digging up gold all day, he will not have time to give me my lessons, so I am going to start school tomorrow. I think it will be fun, to learn with other children. And last night Vati asked Signor Carboni if he would teach me Italian. I am to have my first lesson this afternoon.

Now Mama is beating the batter for suet dumplings, to put in with the mutton. I asked her this morning if she still minds about living here, and she said, 'Well, *liebchen*, we cannot walk back to Melbourne through all that mud.'

Monday 10 July

Mama was going to take me to school. I had my one shilling and sixpence (that is the fee for the week) tied up in a clean handkerchief, and Signor Carboni had written down how to get there:

> *Go down the Melbourne Road, past the Eureka Hotel.*
> *Turn left onto Eureka field and look for big tent with*
> *NATIONAL SCHOOL in black letters.*

But after Mama made the men's breakfasts this morning (four fried chops each as well as damper and a pannikin of tea) she was sick behind the woodpile, and had to lie down. She still insisted she would take me, but when Sal arrived at our camp site, I said I would go with her.

When I got there, Mr Cadwallader (he's the teacher) said to sit next to my friend. That was lucky, I thought, because to tell you the truth, Jennychen, I was feeling very shy. (On my other side there was a girl with hair the colour of carrots. She gave me a nasty look, as if I had done something spiteful to her.)

It is *so* different from having lessons just with you and Laura, or alone with Vati! You cannot imagine what it is like to be in a room (well, a tent) with forty or fifty other children aged from about six years old to the big boys of thirteen. It seems stupid to me, but everyone is made to sit in classes according to age. I think Mr Cadwallader should put people together according to what they know, and then teach them what they don't know.

He gave me this book called the *Fourth Book*, and asked me if I could try to read a certain passage. It was so simple that even Laura would have found it babyish. And it was such a *bad* poem about a robin redbreast that when I finished, I found myself saying the William Blake couplet. (You know: 'A Robin Redbreast in a Cage/Puts all Heaven in a Rage.') But Mr Cadwallader stared at me and said, 'That isn't in the passage.' I could swear he thought I'd made it up. Everyone else was looking at me—even Sal—as if I were a loony.

We were let out for dinner at 12 o'clock. Mama wasn't here when I got back because she had taken the food to the men at our goldmine. (That is about half a mile away.) The fire had nearly gone out, and when I went to put more wood on, there was a snake in the woodpile. So I didn't do anything. And then the fire did go out and Mama sighed when she came back. She has been appointed the tentkeeper of our goldmining party, which means that she has to fetch the water and keep the fire going and buy the food and cook it and guard the gold (when the others dig it up). In most parties there are only men, so they take it in turns to be tentkeeper. J J says we are lucky to have a lady tentkeeper in our party.

Sal and I went back to school at 2 o'clock. We got there a bit early and the carrot-haired girl from our class was organising a ball game with the other girls, but they didn't throw the ball to Sal or me although we stood in the circle. Most of the girls don't wear boots—they walk barefoot through the puddles! And they wear their skirts pinned up around their waists to keep them clean, but of course they have mud caked all over their flannel petticoats. (Sal wears boots, like me. Did I tell you she has the thickest golden plait, and she flicks it across her shoulder in a very stylish fashion?)

This afternoon there was Geography. That was so easy too. Mr Cadwallader asked questions around the class, starting with the most simple ones for the First Class and working up to harder ones for the Fifth Class.

Would you believe that some of the big boys couldn't even find Paris on the map? But everyone knew the answer to 'What is the chief product of California?'

'GOLD GOLD GOLD GOLD GOLD GOLD GOLD GOLD!' They all waved their arms in the air and yelled.

(That is a strange thing. When you want to answer a question, you have to wave your arm in the air, as if you are swatting a fly. This morning I was in trouble for just saying an answer, as I would if Vati asked me a question. I feel it will take me a while to learn the rules about school. Some of them are written on a board hung from the tent pole—like NO SHOUTING NO SPITTING NO SWEARING—but I fear that most of the rules are not written down and I will just have to work them out for myself.)

Apart from the invisible rules, school seemed simple. But then the last hour of the afternoon (we go until 5 o'clock) was—guess what?

Yes—Needlework!

Mrs Cadwallader came in to supervise the girls (the boys did drawing) and we had to sew samplers. She gave me a fresh piece of canvas for mine. Each girl's sampler has the alphabet up the top, then the numbers from 1 to 20, and then a little passage from the Bible. Sal is already halfway through embroidering her text. (Did I tell you her father is a Preacher? Well, on Sundays. He digs for gold during the week, like all the other men.) Mrs Cadwallader offered to help me choose my passage, but I told her my parents do not agree with Religion. She went quite pink in the face and made a spluttery sound, but all she said was that I could just start by doing the letters of the alphabet.

Anyway, I am the worst in the whole school at Needlework. I am worse than the little girls in First Class. And I am even worse than the girl with carrot-coloured hair, who wouldn't throw the ball to Sal and me at dinnertime. I have discovered that her name is Katie Flanagan. She has two younger sisters at the school (you can pick them all by their hair) and after school I watched them head off across the Eureka field. (I was going home alone because Sal stayed back to help Mrs Cadwallader put the sewing things away.)

These are gold nuggets. I am determined to find some.

I HAVE DRAWN YOU A MAP
SO YOU CAN SEE WHERE I LIVE!

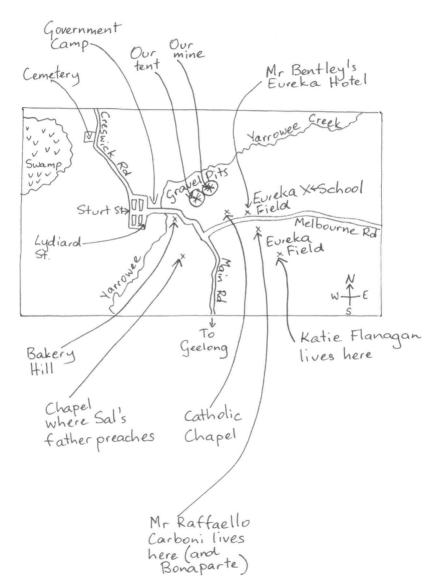

Thursday 13 July 1854

I have got a job of my very own! At breakfast today (fried mutton chops as usual), J J asked if I would like to be in charge of Tulip, and take her every night to the grazing land across the creek, then go early each morning to bring her to the mine.

Mama said, 'Something terrible might happen to her.' (She meant to me, not to Tulip. There are a lot of Vandemonian cutthroats around. Or it is easy to fall down an old mine.)

Vati said, 'I think Rosa should start to learn responsibility.'

And I said, 'I would love to look after Tulip!' (Even though I am still a little bit nervous of horses, I would like to be a member of the gold-digging party.)

So after school I went to the mine. Tulip had finished her last load for the day (she takes the washdirt from the mine to the creek), and J J unharnessed her from the dray. Then we tied on the halter rope and led her across the creek (it is called the Yarrowee) to a wide-open field with good grass. There J J taught me how to put the hobbles around Tulip's ankles so that she does not stray in the night.

As we were leaving, I saw the three Flanagan girls arrive, each one riding bareback on a horse, and leading another horse. They reminded me of the riders in Mrs

Rowe's American Circus. J J says that some children earn money by looking after horses.

'Will I earn money by looking after Tulip?' I asked.

J J laughed, and said I would have to ask my father.

I know what Vati would say! (Never mind. I still wear my Chinese charm around my neck, and I am determined to find some gold of my very own, before very long.)

'You'll be all right with Tulip,' J J assured me as we walked back over the stepping stones, across the creek.

But I am scared that when I go to get her tomorrow morning, she won't want to come to me. Or even worse—she'll have been stolen by Vandemonian horse thieves, and I will not be able to find her.

Friday 14 July, 1854
Weather: fine but a bit cold (especially at dawn when the frost is on the grass)

Last night, before I went into the tent, I wished upon my special wishing stars that Tulip would be easy to catch. And when I went to get her this morning, she came straight to me as soon as I called. (Mama had given me a lump of sugar to hold in my hand, so maybe that helped!) I managed to take the hobbles off in only three attempts, and then I put the halter on.

Katie Flanagan was there, with her sisters Maeve

and Colleen, but they didn't say anything when I called out 'Hello!' I know they were busy catching the six horses that they look after, but I do think they really hate me, and I do not know why. I expect it is because I have broken one of the invisible rules of school.

By the time I got Tulip to the mine, my father and the other men had arrived. Poor Vati! His hands are so blistered that the skin is hanging in shreds, so he is going to work the cradle down at the creek today with Sancho Panza, and J J and Alphonse are going to stay at the mine and take turns with the digging and the windlass. They haven't found any gold yet. (J J says it can take some months before they 'bottom'. That means to get to the bottom, where the gold lies waiting in the ancient dried up river bed.)

By the time I got back to our camp, I was too late to walk to school with Sal, so I went by myself. Then at dinnertime Sal stayed back to clean the slates for the teacher, so I had to walk home again by myself.

So now I have no friends in Ballarat (except for Boney and Tulip). I wish you were here, Jennychen, and we would go looking for gold together, and make our fortunes.

At least today is the last day of school for the week. I am already sick to death of the *Fourth Book*. It is so boring.

Today is Bastille Day, so Alphonse has invited some of the other Frenchmen at the diggings to come to our camp to celebrate. Mama is sighing as she tries to cook a sort of sultana cake in the camp oven. But I know she does not really mind. Alphonse makes her laugh.

This is a gumleaf that I pressed for you.

Wednesday 19 July 1854

Mama and I are making a red and gold flag to fly from our tent, and another one to fly from the top of the windlass at the mine. That will be our address. When I make friends, I will be able to say, 'Come and visit! I live on the Gravel Pits, at the tent with the gold and scarlet pennant!'

(Did I tell you that when I went exploring the other day, I found a Chinese shop like the one in Melbourne? Except that this one was in a tent. On the counter, there were all sorts of mysterious things in big glass jars.)

Friday 21 July 1854

As I came home from school at dinnertime, I saw a wedding at the Chapel where Sal's father preaches. The bride had a bouquet of gumleaves, and a wreath of wildflowers in her hair. The bridegroom is one of the Cornishmen who have come across from South Australia. Vati says they dig burrows through the earth, like moles.

Thank heavens that school is finished for another week! And my parents have promised that some sort of surprise will happen tonight. I cannot imagine what it may be!

Saturday 22 July 1854

I am so happy, Jennychen! Last night's surprise turned out to be a visit to the Gravel Pits Theatre, to see Miss Clara du Val. (Isn't that the most wonderful name? I have decided that when I am a famous actress I am going to change my name to something exotic.) The performance was called SHAKESPEARE'S HEROINES, and Miss du Val just stood on the stage by herself in a long white robe with different coloured cloaks or shawls, and first she was Titania, and next she was Portia, then Miranda, then Ophelia, then Kate from the *Shrew* . . . But the best bit of all was when she did Lady Macbeth. Her wild black hair was hanging down, and she had a red velvet cloak on, and she was holding a bloody dagger in her hand—and I could feel the chills running up and down my spine, as she plotted murder!

Ballarat may be a long way from London and Paris, but even my father agreed that you could not find a more blood-curdling Lady Macbeth anywhere in the whole of Europe!

Sunday 23 July 1854

Just back from my third Italian lessson with Signor Carboni. We had not long started when dear Boney began barking to announce the arrival of one of Signor Carboni's friends—whom I recognised instantly as the Priest who lives beside the Chapel at the border of our field and the Eureka field. Every Sunday morning I see a lot of the Eureka people going there (including Katie and her sisters).

I immediately got up to leave of course, but my teacher laughed and said that Father Pat would love to join our conversation class. (That was how Signor Carboni said his name. I have heard other people call him 'Father Smyth'.)

At first I felt very shy, but Father Pat has such a lively face (I think he is quite young—I mean, for an adult), and was so busy smiling or laughing or asking unexpected questions, that soon I felt as if I had known him for years.

'How did you learn Italian?' I asked him. (In Italian, of course. Signor Carboni will not allow me to use English in class.)

Father Pat explained that he did some of his training in Rome. 'But why are *you* learning Italian, in Ballarat?' he asked me.

So I explained to him that I am having a competition with my best friend in London to see who can learn the most languages by the time we are twelve.

'You should try Latin,' the Priest suggested.

I told him that my father had promised to teach me when we got to Ballarat, but now he is always busy digging for gold, or else he is too tired.

Then, guess what, Jennychen? Father Pat offered to teach me Latin. He said I could come to his hut for lessons on Saturday mornings. 'Better ask your parents first,' he said. 'Perhaps they would not like it.'

I think I was secretly hoping that when I told Vati, he would say he didn't want me to be visiting a Priest, and then he would offer to teach me himself. But he just said, 'Good idea, *liebchen*. I have heard that Father Patrick Smyth is a fine classical scholar.'

It is funny how I seem to be good at making friends with grown-ups here in Ballarat, and with horses and dogs, but I still do not have any other children to play with. Sal is nice enough, but she likes to sit in the tent and keep her clothes clean, and when I offered her the role of maid in my Judith play, she said her father says that the theatre is one of the Devil's playgrounds. (I told her Judith is in the Bible, and she said that probably made it worse.)

Monday 27 July 1854
Weather: cold, drizzle

Something dreadful just happened, Jennychen. Something so unexpected—it is hard to describe it.

I was coming home from school for my dinner (Sal stayed back to help Mrs Cadwallader get the materials ready for the Needlework lesson) and as I approached the Gravel Pits I heard the cry 'Joe! Joe!' coming from all sides. I naturally thought that there was some man called 'Joe', whom all the diggers were looking for. And then over the thumping of the cradles and the clanking of the windlass buckets, I heard the sound of hoof beats thundering.

I swung around, to see about twenty troopers, riding down the hill from the Government Camp. At the same time, policemen on foot seemed to have appeared from nowhere, all over the Gravel Pits.

'Joe! Joe!' the diggers were shouting, as people might shout 'Fire! Fire!' Some men started clambering down their mine shafts. Some headed for their tents. Many others started running towards the bush, with the troopers on horseback chasing after them as if they were hunting a fox. Meanwhile policemen on foot were grabbing diggers by the collar, threatening them with their muskets and bayonets.

'What on earth is going on?' I wondered.

I was too busy staring to be aware of hoof beats behind me. The next thing I knew, a horse was whinnying, right in my ear. Just as I was about to be ridden down in the chase, I was swung up into the air, out of the way.

'It is too dangerous for you here, little lady,' I heard my rescuer say as he pulled me to safety around the side of a slab hut. For a second I thought it was J J, for the voice had a similar soft drawl, but when I looked at the man's face, I realised that I had never seen him before. He was tall and handsome and was dressed in the usual diggers' clothes, but he had a red sash around his waist.

'What on earth is happening?' I asked him.

He looked almost amused. 'Haven't you seen a digger hunt before?'

'No!' I said. I have never seen anything like it. I can remember what happened in 1848. Vati says I can't, I was too young, but I know I can remember people gathering in the street outside our window, then the soldiers coming, and people shouting and running away. And Mama said we had to pack our bags and go to London . . . I remember that, and it was frightening. But the digger hunt was different, because all the men were busy at their work, and everything was peaceful, and then suddenly the policemen arrived, and started grabbing the diggers, or chasing them.

'What do the police want?' I asked the man with the red sash.

'Licences,' he told me. 'This happens once a month or so. The traps come around, and check that every man has paid for a licence.'

I think I told you, Jennychen, that before Vati started digging he had to buy a licence, permitting him to look for Queen Victoria's gold. He has to buy a new licence every month, whether he finds any gold or not.

My rescuer explained to me that a lot of the diggers cannot afford the thirty shillings to buy a licence every month, because it can take six months or more before they reach the bottom of the shaft, where the gold might be. And in the meantime the miners have to buy food and nobblers and things. (Mama is always saying how terribly expensive everything is here in Ballarat. Even worse than in Melbourne.)

'What happens if the troopers catch a digger and he hasn't got a licence?' I inquired.

But as I asked, my question was already being

answered, for I saw a bluecoat putting the handcuffs onto a digger and chaining him to a log. And as my rescuer escorted me home, I saw this scene repeated up to twenty times.

'What happens to the prisoners?' I asked.

'Once the traps have enough captives, they take them down the gully, to the depot. There will be more down there, that have been caught in the scrub,' the man with the red sash told me. 'Then each prisoner has to give the Commissioner five pounds, for bail money. Those that don't have it are taken up to the Government Camp, to the lockup. After a couple of days in prison, they go before a Magistrate.'

'Joe! Joe!'

'*The traps are out!*'

The cries came from all sides as we hurried through the diggings. And over the shouting could be heard the barking of thousands of dogs, and the occasional bang of a pistol, coming from the scrub.

'That is where we live,' I told my new friend. 'At the tent with the gold and scarlet flag.'

'And a very nice flag it looks, too,' he remarked.

As we approached, Mama ran out and hugged me. I could tell she had been afraid.

'Oh, Mama!' I told her. 'I was nearly squashed by a horse. But this man saved me.'

'How can I ever thank you?' my mother asked the man with the red sash.

'Think nothing of it!' My rescuer took off his hat with a flourish and bowed. 'At your service, Ma'am . . .' And then he was gone, before Mama could ask his name.

Now it is a couple of hours later, and I am writing to you because Mama said she did not want me going back to school this afternoon. (That is the only good thing—I have missed Needlework!)

The licence hunt is finally over. I have seen the prisoners being marched like a chain gang of convicts back towards the Government Camp. But they are not criminals. They are free men.

Soon I will go to where Vati is digging, and collect Tulip. I am so pleased that my father has a licence, or else he might be in prison now.

Saturday 29 July 1854

Had my first Latin lesson this morning!

Father Pat's servant was there too, and was polishing the candlesticks while the lesson was going on. He is from Armenia, and is called Joannes, and he does not speak very much English. (I wonder if it would be difficult to learn Armenian.)

Already I know that I like Latin very much. It is so

neat and orderly. Father Pat gave me the words for the numbers, and the verb 'To Be', and a few nouns and pronouns and adjectives, and by the end of the lesson I was able to make little sentences!

Puella sum:	I am a girl.
Malus est:	He is bad.
Pater meus bonus est:	My father is good.
Liber parvus est:	The book is small.
Mensa magna est:	The table is big.

At the end of the lesson, the Priest read me some Julius Caesar, who is one of his favourite Latin authors. Of course, I couldn't understand the words, but it was like poetry to hear them read by Father Pat's Irish voice.

By next week I have to memorise the vocabulary, and translate some more sentences. Easy! (Father Pat has lent me a red Grammar Book, small enough to fit in my pocket.)

Tuesday 1 August 1854
Weather: fine

A new month has begun, so at dinnertime today Mama and I set off to the Government Camp, to buy new licences for Vati and the rest of our party. We walked through the Gravel Pits to Bakery Hill, where we joined the Main Road, and then proceeded across the little bridge that spans the Yarrowee. (Mama had the thirty shillings for each man's licence tied up tightly in her pocket, in case any Vandemonians attacked us on the way.)

But when at last we took the turn to the Camp, we could see that the licence queue stretched from the Gold Commissioner's tent, all the way down the road. There must have been close to a thousand men (and a few women), waiting to buy licences. Mama decided to come back early tomorrow.

As we had walked all the way there through the mud we decided to do our shopping up in the Town, instead of at the shops on the Gravel Pits. When I say 'shops', Jennychen, you are not to imagine stone or brick buildings like the stores in London or Paris. The shops on the diggings are just tents or bark huts. Inside you will see the greatest higgledy-piggledy array of cheeses, candle wax, bloaters, bolts of cloth, dried figs, ladies' wigs, spices, gunpowder and shot, Wellington boots, blankets, rope, sewing twine, tents of all sizes, turpentine, ironmongery, washing soda, waterproof coats, arrowroot—all piled together. Never of course any fresh vegetables or fruit. (The only things we have with our mutton are potatoes and sometimes onions, if we are lucky. Plus of course damper, and sometimes dumplings.)

The worst shops are the butchers' shambles. They

really make me sick. And Mama goes green when we have to get the meat. The farmers around the diggings sell off their skinniest oldest jumbucks (that is what sheep are called in the Colony). Then the butchers chop them into quarters and leave all the inside bits lying around for the dogs to fight over. It is not hot enough yet for there to be many flies, but another lady told Mama to just wait. When the summer starts, you sometimes cannot see the meat for the overcoat of flies crawling all over it.

Mutton mutton mutton mutton. That is all there ever is. Unless J J goes out with his gun on a Sunday afternoon and gets some cockatoos. (They are a type of parroquet.) Last week Alphonse made cockatoo pie, but I would not eat any. Mama did not either. (She is still often sick.)

But today she was well, and we had a good time (except for not getting the licences). Some of the shops in the little Township are real buildings, and there is an Arcade being built in Lydiard Street. We even joined the circulating library. Mama borrowed a copy of the latest Charles Dickens, and I got *Children of the New Forest*, by Captain Marryat. Imagine a book by my dear Captain Marryat finding its way to the Antipodes! The man who runs the library told Mama that there are a number of reading groups here at the diggings, and perhaps she might like to join one.

'Or even start one,' Mama said.

I would very much like it, if our family joined a reading group. I am so sick of the *Fourth Book*. But at least now I have Alice, Edith, Edward and Humphrey as my companions. (They of course are the Beverley children, who live in the New Forest. Have you read it, Jennychen?)

And guess who we saw at the library? Lady Macbeth! She was looking ever so elegant in a blue silken gown.

On the way home I made Mama take a detour through the Chinese part of the diggings, so that we could see the shop with the funny things in jars. She told me that they are medicines, and the man is a special Chinese doctor.

'Why don't you go in?' I suggested.

'Because I am not ill, *liebchen*,' she smiled at me.

But I think that she is.

Thursday 3 August 1854

Unus, duo, tres, quattuor, quinque, sex, septem, octo, novem, decem . . .

This evening I was practising the Latin numbers on Tulip, as I took her to the creek paddock, and Katie Flanagan heard me! No wonder she thinks I am stupid.

Undecim, duodecim, tredecim, quattuordecim, quindecim, sedecim, septemdecim . . .

You should see Katie riding her piebald mare. She can even stand up on her horse's back, like the performers from Mrs Rowe's American Circus.

Monday 7 August 1854

Needlework this afternoon was insufferable. I stabbed myself so badly with my needle that I got blood all over my sampler. Mrs Cadwallader made me sit down the front with the girls in the First Grade, and little Colleen Flanagan started them all giggling at me. I am still only halfway through stitching the letters of the alphabet. I am doing them alternately in scarlet and gold thread and I think they look stylish. (Besides, the blood does not show when it is on the scarlet.) Sal and most of the other girls use pale colours like pink and lavender and lemon. Mrs C was asking me again if I have chosen a Bible text to embroider, but I just shook my head. I have found out that she runs the Sunday School at the Chapel where Sal's father preaches. That is probably why she makes a special pet of Sal. Mr Cadwallader does too. I can see now why Katie Flanagan and all the other girls do not like Sal. But the trouble is—they think that I am Sal's friend, and so they will not play with me either.

Oh, Jennychen, I so miss my lessons just with you

and Laura. Trying to make friends with a lot of girls is very complicated.

At least I have something good to look forward to tonight. My parents are holding the first meeting of our reading group. I wonder what novel we will start with. Anything will be wonderful, after the *Fourth Book*!

And doing Latin always makes me feel better. These are some of the sentences I am writing for this week's homework:

Scutum magnum est:	The shield is big.
Frater meus parvus est:	My brother is little.
Hortus venustus est:	The garden is lovely.
Hic equus amicus meus est:	This horse is my friend.

I wish we could do Latin at school, instead of Needlework. (Except I suppose it would not be the same, without Father Pat.)

Tuesday 8 August 1854

I am so cross with my father. Our reading group is not going to have a novel that we can all listen to as people take turns in reading. Oh no! Vati has announced that the group will study books of Political Economy. (He even brought out some of your father's work, Jennychen.) The people who came were all men. One was called Mr

Humffray, and there were two brothers called Mr Black, and a black man called Mr Joseph. Then there was Mr Thonen (who sells lemonade from a cart). And Raffy (who at least brought my darling Bonaparte). Besides that, there was of course our usual group around the campfire—J J and Sancho Panza and Alphonse.

I think Mama is as disappointed as I am. And of course the reading group was her idea.

Afterwards, I heard Vati telling her that Mr Humffray and the Black brothers are Chartists. I thought he meant they made maps, but this morning when I asked him, he explained that the Chartists are an English political society about Democracy.

I do not care what they are. They are all as boring as your father's friends, Jennychen, when they get together and talk about Politics.

(Thank heavens for dear Captain Marryat and the children of the New Forest. At least I was able to escape for a while with the Beverleys.)

Monday 14 August 1854

Sal saw me going into Father Pat's hut on Saturday morning and now she is not talking to me. She says her father says that she is not allowed to speak to Papists.

I said, 'I do not see how the Pope has anything to do with my Latin lesson.'

'The Pope speaks Latin,' Sal replied, as if that proved something.

'So did Julius Caesar,' I told her.

But Sal just tossed her plait and walked away.

When I told Vati, he said that Salvation should not be blamed for her father's opinions.

To tell you the truth, Jennychen, I do not mind at all that Sal does not want to speak to me. I am getting along very happily with my new friends, Alice, Edith, Edward and Humphrey. When I take Tulip to the creek I pretend that she is a New Forest pony like the ones that the Beverley children ride. (Did I tell you that I now ride Tulip, instead of leading her? I have no saddle of course, and I hitch up my skirt and sit astride, like a boy.)

Needlework was abominable again. My sampler is now as bloody as Lady Macbeth's gown.

Saturday 19 August 1854

When I arrived at Father Pat's place this morning for my Latin lesson, Katie Flanagan and her two little sisters were leaving.

'What're *you* doing here?' Katie asked. As if I didn't have a right to be there.

'What're *you* doing here?' I asked her back.

'We have Catechism class with Father Pat,' Colleen Flanagan replied.

'You can't do Catechism,' Maeve Flanagan told me. 'You're not a Catholic.'

'Nor was Julius Caesar!' I shouted at her. I was sick to death of being told what I was or what I wasn't, by people like Salvation Jones and Maeve Flanagan.

It was at that point that the Priest stepped out of the little bark Chapel. 'Girls, girls!' he said. 'What is all this about Julius Caesar?'

I do not know how much he had heard. Katie went bright pink, as if she thought she would be in trouble, but her little sisters were oblivious.

'She's saying that Julius Caesar wasn't a Catholic,' Colleen reported.

'Well, that is very true,' Father Pat said. 'And neither was our Lord Jesus Christ. He was a Jew.' The Priest smiled at me. 'Like our friend Rosa here.'

The Flanagans stared. At me. At Father Pat.

'Off you go now, girls,' the Priest told the Flanagans. 'I am sure that your mother needs you for something. Rosa and I have to further our acquaintance with Julius Caesar.'

Katie gave me a strange look as they walked away. I do not know if Father Pat really helped me, or if Katie Flanagan will hate me even more now.

Monday 21 August 1854
Weather: a fine night, with lots of stars
(including my special wishing stars)

Exercitus magnus est: The army is big.
Bellum longum erit et triste: The war will be long and sad.
Milites semper violenti erunt: Soldiers will always be violent.

Last Thursday's *Argus* arrived today, and now Vati's reading group is arguing so loudly that I cannot think to do my Latin homework, so I will write to you instead, Jennychen. (Your letter came last week. I am glad that you received the one I posted from the boat. That seems so long ago now! As there is no point to writing plays any more, without anyone to act in them, it is good to have you to write to.)

Not much news. I am still loving Latin and Italian, and it is easy to learn them together, because so many words do for both. And besides, it is always fun to visit Raffy and Boney, and Father Pat and Joannes. (Raffy is here now of course, at the reading group. When he argues, he waves his arms around and gets so excited that it is funny to watch.)

I have finished *The Children of the New Forest*, and am reading it for a second time. It is strange that the Beverley children and their family are Royalists, and

Cromwell and the Republicans are the enemy. Here in Upside Down Land, that too is reversed. My father and his friends are always talking about how the Colony should be a Republic. Here the Royalists are the police and soldiers—and of course the Governor.

That is who the men are talking about now. He made a speech at a banquet in Geelong last week, and now Vati and Mr Humffray and Mr Joseph and Raffy and the lemonade man are arguing about whether the Governor really meant what he said.

'No,' says Vati. 'I have told you—Charles Hotham is a complete despot.'

'Perhaps he has changed,' Mr Joseph suggests. (He always likes to think the best of everybody.)

'It seems that he has,' Mr Humffray agrees. He picks up the newspaper again and reads it, to make sure. 'Listen! *All power proceeds from the people.* That is what the Governor said in Geelong last Wednesday. He even said that he intends to conduct his administration according to that principle.'

'Maybe,' say the two brothers called Mr Black. 'Maybe he really is a new broom who is going to sweep clean.'

'More likely it is just a lot of yabber yabber!' Raffy announces, and passes around the bottle of nobbler.

'Perhaps we will be able to see for ourselves soon,

when the Governor makes his tour of the goldfields,' says Mama, who is sitting sewing at the edge of the fire.

Oh! There is some news that I do not think I have told you. There is going to be a baby in our family. That is why Mama is making the tiniest little white nightgown I have ever seen. She says I was once small enough to have worn it, but I am sure that she is wrong. Her stitches are so beautiful that even Mrs Cadwallader would not be able to match them. (I was in trouble again in Needlework today. And I still do not have a passage to embroider . . . But I have just had such a clever idea, Jennychen!)

Saturday 26 August 1854
Weather: morning fine. Afternoon deluge!

This afternoon there was the most enormous rainstorm, when I was riding Tulip to the creek paddock. Just as I was sloshing back through the mud into the Gravel Pits, I heard a lot of shouting coming from behind the Ballarat Dining Room. (That is a large tent, set up as a restaurant. We never eat there because Mama says it is not a place for women and children. Though it is not nearly so bad as the Eureka Hotel. Mama says that I must not even walk on that side of the road because of all the men who have drunk too many nobblers. A lot of soldiers drink there.)

When I heard the noise behind the Dining Room, naturally I ran up to see what was happening. Spying a great many men crowded around a mine shaft, I thought that someone must have discovered a huge nugget. But when I wriggled my way to the front of the circle, I saw my old enemy.

No, not Mrs Cadwallader. Sir Charles Hotham! The man who caused me such trouble on the ship. (To tell you the truth, I had forgotten that he was due to arrive in Ballarat today.) Seeing the crowd, and remembering what Vati had said so long ago about how the Governor was going to cause trouble on the diggings too, I wondered: *Is that going to happen now?* But as I glanced around, I immediately realised that everyone was smiling and cheering, and Sir Charles and Lady Hotham were smiling back.

'Speech! Speech!' someone shouted, so the Governor climbed up onto a stump and thanked the diggers for the opportunity to inspect their place of work. 'I feel delighted with your reception,' he added, 'And I assure you that I will not neglect your interests and welfare.'

The men started cheering again, and some called out that he was 'The Diggers' Charley'.

As the Governor and Lady Hotham began to make their way back to the Government Camp, a great many of the diggers ran ahead, laying slabs of wood down on the muddy road, to make a footpath. At one point there was such a huge crab-hole in the road that a man known as Big Larry lifted Lady Hotham up in his arms and carried her over it, and everyone laughed and cheered again. The Governor even laughed back, as if he were an ordinary man, and not a Royalist despot.

It was then that I was aware of my father, standing silent in the crowd, watching. I went up to him and took his hand, but he seemed barely to notice that I was there. I remembered what he said on the ship, about Governor Hotham causing trouble. It seems strange to me that my father's judgement should be so wrong.

This is Judith's dagger.

Sunday 27 August 1854
Weather: cloudy

Last night I dreamed the strangest dream.

I cannot remember how it began, but I was here at the diggings, and when I looked up into the sky, I saw the blue suddenly clouded out by the white wings of a huge bird which seemed to hover for an eternity above

Ballarat. It just hung, as an eagle might hang upon the wind currents, picking out its prey.

Then there were bangs, and suddenly a licence hunt was swirling around me—there were Joes everywhere, and soldiers too on horseback—and as another gun went off, I heard a terrible sound like a roaring wind, and I looked up and saw the albatross falling out of the sky and down down, it plummeted down and landed at my feet, all bloody.

. . . This morning I found a white feather near the woodpile. I knew that was just a coincidence, but it brought back the dream and made me feel anxious. So I threw the feather into the fire, where it made a horrid smell. I feel as if I can still smell it, as I write this.

Monday 4 September
Weather: golden. Wattle everywhere. (It is the beginning of Spring in Upside Down Land!)

Oh Jennychen, what a day! I am so tired but so excited, I must at least start to write this down (although I fear I may fall asleep before I finish. It is reading group again tonight of course, so it will be a while before my parents come to bed.) To tell you the truth, I began the morning sick at heart, for I was dreading school even more than I usually do on Mondays. (Last week, when I wrote my passage onto my sampler, Mrs Cadwallader became so furious that I thought she would explode. I told her it was a direct quotation from the Governor of Victoria, but she declared it was a blasphemy. She said that Kings and Queens and Governors rule through the grace of God, and not through the power of the people, and I had to sit in the corner the whole afternoon and darn Mr Cadwallader's smelly old socks.)

SO! You can imagine how I was feeling as I went across the creek this morning to the horse paddock. I could see Maeve and Colleen, and five of the horses that they look after. And I could see my darling Tulip. But I did not see Katie Flanagan. And I did not see the piebald mare, that Katie always rides.

'Rosa! Rosa!' Maeve called to me. 'The Vandemonians have stolen Patchwork.' (That is what the Flanagans call the black and white mare.)

For a moment I wondered: *Are they trying to play a trick on me? If I take them seriously, will Katie ride out from the scrub in triumph, doing some new bareback trick? And then they will all laugh at me!*

'It's true!' Colleen told me. 'There are a lot of horse thieves about.'

I knew she was right. It is common for horses to be stolen. And yet it was possible too that Patchwork had managed to slip her hobbles, and had wandered off in search of sweeter grazing. I sometimes have to walk a good half-mile before I see Tulip. And she is not nearly as young and frisky as the piebald mare.

And then Katie ran out from the edge of the bush. If she were not Katie Flanagan, I would have thought she was about to weep. 'What shall I do?' she cried. She named the digger who owns that particular horse. He is a big, angry sort of man, whom I often see going into the Eureka Hotel. 'He will make my father pay compensation, if Patchwork is truly lost,' Katie wailed. 'And just this morning Dadda was saying that he does not know how he will pay the licence fee this month.'

'I could help you look for her,' I offered.

'Would you?' Katie seemed surprised.

First, of course, I had to take Tulip up the creek to where Vati and Alphonse were working. Then as soon as my father wasn't looking, I slipped back downstream to meet Katie. Meanwhile Maeve and Colleen had taken the other five horses to their owners.

Katie and I searched through the scrub around the creek, until at last we found Patchwork's hoof-marks. As there were no prints of men's boots, we decided that she must simply have strayed, and not been stolen. What luck!

(Sorry, must stop. Mama is calling to me to blow out the candle and go to sleep. She does not know anything about today of course!)

There are many snakes around the diggings.

Tuesday 5 September 1854

Morning

I will try to finish the story as I eat my breakfast (damper and dripping) . . .

SO—we set off through the bush—following Patchwork's hoof-prints. If we had not been so anxious it would have been a pretty walk, for the wattle is flowering, and also other wildflowers. But we were in too much of a hurry to look at them.

We searched on and on, following the hoof-marks, losing them, then picking up the trail again, as we made our way over hills covered thickly with gum trees. Meanwhile the sun rose higher and higher in the sky, and we became hotter and thirstier, for we had long since left the creek.

When did we realise that we had lost Patchwork's track?

And when did we realise that we too were lost?

By then the sun was right overhead.

Will have to finish this at dinnertime! I have to go and get Tulip. I just hope the horses are all there today!

Dinnertime
Joes! Joes! Police are appearing all around the Gravel Pits as I try to write this. It is strange to have a hunt so early in the month. Thank goodness Vati has a licence. (Mama stood in line at the Government Camp all day yesterday and bought him a new one.)

But to continue my story—Yes! We did not know where on earth we were!

I cannot tell you, Jennychen, how terrifying the Australian bush can be, when you are lost in it. In England, you know that you can always climb a tree and see a Church spire, and know where the nearest Village is. Here—it seems that there is nothing. Just miles and miles of trees and trees and trees, as endless as the ocean. The only sound is the jackass, laughing as if to mock you.

If I had not had Katie with me, I think I would have sat down and howled.

Now Mama says I must stop my journal. She is determined that she will walk me back to school, because the traps are out.

Night

Something terrible has happened, which I must tell you before I continue the story of being Lost in the Australian Bush.

As Mama and I were walking through the Eureka field at the end of dinnertime, we saw the Joes chase after a man and catch him, and throw him to the ground.

'Have mercy on him!' Mama cried out, seeing one of the police kick hard with his boot.

And then I realised that the man was Katie's father.

Mama and I hurried to the Flanagans' tent, and told Katie's mother, who began weeping. Their claim has just struck a shicer* (after they have been digging for six whole months) and they do not have the five pounds for the bail money.

'Mama,' I whispered, 'We could lend the Flanagans the money.'

But my mother told me to hush. I was so angry at her. (I still am, as a matter of fact.)

After that, I did not go to school this afternoon, and nor did the Flanagan girls. We played near their tent, while our two mothers drank tea and talked. Mr Flanagan will be forced to stay in the police lockup until the case goes before the magistrate. (Everyone says that the Magistrates are corrupt.)

* A 'shicer' is when you get right down to the old dried up creek bed, where you expect the gold to be—and there isn't any there!

Saturday 9 September 1854

Katie and I have just done our first fossicking expedition! We met at Father Pat's after Katie's Catechism class, and she waited while I did my Latin. Then we collected our equipment and some cold chops and damper, and off we went to the Hidden Valley.

Oh! I realise that I have neglected to tell you about finding the Valley. (So much has been happening, Jennychen!) Well —

On Monday, after Katie and I realised we were lost, Katie remembered her father saying that if you are bushed you should walk downhill, and find a creek, and then follow the water. So we headed down a ridge—and eventually found ourselves in the sweetest little valley, with a small creek running through an open grassland . . .

'Patch!' Katie called, but she did not need to, for the piebald mare came stepping daintily up to us and whinnied softly, as if to welcome us to her secret grazing place.

We had a drink in the little creek, where the water is clear as crystal. (Here in Ballarat the creek water is muddy from all the diggers puddling in it, and Mama has to boil it before we can drink it.) 'Look!' Katie exclaimed, and she pointed out to me the kind of rock that shows that there is gold to be found.

By that time of course it was late afternoon, and there was no time to explore. We clambered up onto Patchwork's back, and let her take us down the little waterway until it joined up with our familiar Yarrowee.

That was Monday. All week we have been itching to get back there and look for gold, so today Katie borrowed one of her father's pans. (He is out of jail now, but has been fined five pounds. Mrs Flanagan had to borrow the money from the publican at the Eureka Hotel, who will make them pay high interest. I still think Mama and Vati should have given them the money.)

Oh Jennychen, it is so much fun to fossick for gold, I can see now why my father caught Gold Fever. I took my stockings and boots off (Katie always wears bare feet) and we took off our skirts and hitched up our petticoats, and then we dug the soil from the creek bank and washed it in our pan.

Perhaps I should explain that the pan is a shallow dish, and you put a scoop of dirt in, and then some water, and you swirl it around until you wash off the dirt—the feeling of anticipation is quite delicious. Then the gold dust settles at the bottom of the pan.

Well. That is how it is meant to happen. We did not actually find any today, but I know that we will.

Have to stop in a minute.* Mama is dishing up the stew (mutton and dumplings). Raffy and the lemonade man are here for supper tonight. I will give some of my mutton to Boney. (He is licking my leg.)

* Learned a really useful phrase in Latin today: *Haec scribens interpellata sum.* It means: 'I am interrupted while I write this.' Or 'I was interrupted while I was writing this.' That always seems to be happening to me!

Monday 11 September 1854

Katie and her sisters are not coming to school any more, because their parents cannot afford to pay. It was so miserable there today, without Katie. Especially in Needlework. (I am putting William Blake on my sampler—the couplet about the robin redbreast. Mrs C will not be able to stop me because Blake is a famous poet.)

I feel as if I have just made a friend, and I am sure to lose her. For now Katie will make friends with all the other children who do not go to school, and she will not want to play with me any more.

Salvation does not speak to me at all. Not that I care.

Thursday 14 September 1854

This afternoon at the creek paddock Katie and Colleen and Maeve and I decided to have a circus. I was telling them about seeing Mrs Rowe's American Circus in the parade in Melbourne, and Colleen said how she wished it would come to Ballarat.

Then Katie said, 'Why don't we have a circus of our own?'

We have decided to practise our riding tricks and then we will put on a performance, and charge money for tickets, and help Katie's parents pay off their debts. (They owe money to one of the storekeepers as well as the Eureka Hotel man.)

Of course, Katie and I are still going to fossick at the Hidden Valley on Saturdays, but we don't want to take the little girls there. That is our secret. We can practise our circus tricks in the afternoon, when we take the horses to the creek grazing. (It gets dark later now, so I have a couple of hours to play in, after school.)

I am so happy that Katie still wants to be friends.

Saturday 16 September 1854

This morning Katie was waiting for me after her Catechism class, while I did Latin, and Father Pat said to her, 'Why don't you join in?' So now Katie is learning Latin too. We are going to use it as our secret language, so we can talk about our goldmine and no-one will know what we are saying.

We asked Father Pat for some special vocabulary:

gold:	*aurum*
creek:	*flumen*
pan:	*patella*
water:	*aqua*
cool:	*frigidus*
hot:	*fervidus*
valley:	*vallis*

'How do we say "hidden"?' we asked him.

'It depends on what sort of thing you are hiding,' the Priest replied.

'We can't tell you,' we told him.

'Well, you might say *latibulum*. That means "hiding place".'

We added that to our list.

'What is all this about, girls?' Father Pat teased us.

'It is a secret.'

'I am very good at keeping secrets,' Father Pat boasted. But we would not give in!

'*Heus!*' he exclaimed at last. '*Secretum!* Secrecy!'

After Latin we went to the *Latibulum* in the *vallis*, and spent the afternoon at the *flumen*, fossicking for *aurum* with our *patella*. When we are *fervidus*, it is such fun to take our skirts off and puddle in the *aqua frigida* that sometimes I think I don't even mind if we never find any *aurum* (though I know we are going to!).

Tuesday 19 September 1854

The death bell began tolling this morning. There has been another cave-in—this time at one of the Cornishmen's mines. People say it is especially dangerous, the way they burrow like moles through the earth, but if truth be told, all goldmining is dangerous. Cave-ins are common, and this is not the first time someone has died since we have been here.

Of course, every time something happens, all the women fear for their own husbands. At dinnertime, Mama was looking troubled.

As if that were not bad enough, there was another licence hunt this afternoon. And on the way back from the creek paddock, Katie and I saw a new contingent of traps and troopers coming up the Melbourne Road.

'*Exercitus magnus est!*' Katie observed.

'*Milites semper violenti erunt,*' I agreed.

'What are you two saying?' Maeve and Colleen were desperate to know.

'*Secretum!*' Katie said to me, and looked mysterious.

Wednesday 20 September
Morning

Last night I heard my parents talking quietly in the tent, long after the candle was blown out.

'What are we going to do?' Mama asked. Then she changed into Yiddish, which always makes her more comfortable. 'What are we going to do for money?'

Vati promised her that he and the other men are sure to find gold soon.

'How soon?'

'How can I answer that?'

'And in the meantime we are virtually penniless!'

I wanted to cry out in the darkness, 'Don't worry! Katie and I have found a rich new place to dig!' But we want to find some nuggets before we tell our parents. And besides, if I said anything, then Mama would know that I had overheard what they were talking about, and she would worry more. (My boots are starting to feel tight, but I dare not tell Mama. New boots cost a FORTUNE in Ballarat.)

I know that we were often without money in

Europe, and also in London—and I know that your father too is often penniless. But Mama seems to find it worse here, where she has no friends she can talk to in the way she used to talk to your mother.

Evening
There was yet another licence hunt today, and all the adults are saying how it is unfair for the Joes to come out twice in one week.

Thursday 21 September 1854
Coming home from school at dinnertime I heard the drum beating for the funeral of that poor digger who died on Tuesday. And when the cortège went past, there at the head of the procession was the young bride that I saw, only a couple of months ago. The one that had wildflowers in her hair. Now there were more wildflowers on the coffin lid, and a wreath of gumleaves. People say her name is Mrs Tredinnick. She is really pretty.

Saturday 23 September 1854
At Latin class this morning, Joannes Gregorius came in and started darning one of Father Pat's long black robes. He was muttering in Armenian and it didn't sound as if he was enjoying sewing very much. (I know how he feels!)

Had a great day today at the *Latibulum*. I think we

nearly found some *aurum*.

When we came back there was another licence hunt going on. These days the soldiers ride through the diggings, as well as the mounted police. As Katie and I were passing Big Larry's claim we saw the traps grabbing him and demanding to see his licence. It took four of them to hold him. He spat upon the ground and shouted, 'I give you *that* for the Digger's Charley.' He spat again. 'And *that* for his fair lady!' It is strange to think that it is only a few weeks since the Governor was here, and Big Larry was carrying Lady Hotham, and everyone was cheering. (Except for my father.)

Haec scribens interpellata sum! I told Mama about Joannes Gregorius, and now she wants me to run down to the Chapel and tell Father Pat that she would be happy to do his sewing for him, to thank him for my Latin lessons.

Tuesday 26 September 1854

We have a new flag flying from our tent. Well, this is really more of a sign. Mama used a brush and some of Vati's best Chinese ink to write onto a piece of canvas:

SEWING

TAILORING

DRESSMAKING

DARNING

SHIRTMAKING
REPAIRS
NO JOB TOO BIG!
NO JOB TOO SMALL!
APPLY WITHIN!

Another licence hunt today. All the adults are very cross. Some of Vati's mates are here tonight, and they are sitting around the fire grumbling.

Our circus is getting better and better. Some of the Hayes children have joined it too. (They live on Eureka, close to Katie's family. I often see Mr and Mrs Hayes when I visit the Flanagans.) And I am going to ask Raffy if we can borrow Boney, to do tricks.

Sunday 1 October 1854
Weather: getting hotter

There is never anyone to play with on Sunday mornings because Katie and the Hayeses are at Mass. You should see the huge crowd around the little Chapel—more than a thousand people go every week. I wait until I hear the last bell before I go down there and meet the others. And then we all go to the creek paddock and start circus practice.

There are ten of us now—six Hayeses, three Flanagans and me. We are thinking of a name—like

'Mrs Rowe's American Circus', but different. Danny Hayes suggested 'Father Pat's Irish Circus' (Father Pat has agreed to be our Patron), but Katie said it would have to be 'Irish and Jewish', to include me.

As well as the Equestrian events, we are training Boney to jump through hoops (we don't set them on fire). And Danny is teaching himself to juggle.

I still do Italian with Raffy on Sunday afternoons, after circus practice. Katie comes to that too.

Haec scribens interpellata sum . . . There's the last Mass bell, so I have to go!

Saturday 7 October 1854
Weather: hot, with sticky flies buzzing everywhere

Morning

There has been a murder, Jennychen! Not far from the Eureka Hotel. All the men are talking about it. Mama has sent me into the tent to write up my journal so that I cannot hear, but already I have heard Sancho Panza and Alphonse discussing it as they ate their breakfast. It was a digger called Mr Scobie who got killed. People are saying that, about an hour past midnight, he and a mate went to the Eureka Hotel to try to buy a drink, but the owner (Mr Bentley) sent them away. A few minutes later, out in the darkness, poor Mr Scobie was bashed on the head. Everyone thinks it was Bentley himself who followed Scobie and hit him on the head.

The men will be setting off to work soon, so I must go and get Tulip. I cannot wait to talk to Katie about it.

Just think! Mama always told me that it was dangerous to go near the Eureka Hotel.

Night

Went exploring up the creek in the *Latibulum* this afternoon, panning as we went. Did not actually find any gold dust, but we saw lots and lots of fluffy golden wattle, and caught some tiny fishes in our pan. We also saw some bright red and green parrots, and a kingfisher with a blue velvet waistcoat.

Anyway, if we had discovered gold it would not be a good time to tell our parents tonight, because all the adults are talking about the Inquest that happened this afternoon. The Court just decided that Mr Scobie was killed by a blow on the head by Somebody Unknown. A lot of the diggers are angry because they think Mr Bentley should be charged with murder.

Danny Hayes knows a boy who lives with his mother in a tent near where the body was found. And he says that this boy heard Mr and Mrs Bentley's voices in the night, just at the time when the crime would have happened.

Danny is getting good at juggling. He can keep three potatoes in the air at the same time!

Tuesday 10 October 1854
Weather: hot with a north wind

Katie and I are upset because our friend Joannes Gregorius is in trouble. At dinner time today I did not go home, but went to the Flanagans' tent for play practice. (We have decided to do the Judith play as part of the circus. Raffy has agreed to be the wicked king Holofernes. We are now calling ourselves 'The Irish, Jewish and Italian Equestrian and Theatrical Circus.') Anyway, Katie and I were reading through our parts (she is the maid) and her mother asked us to take a kettle of broth to a poor neighbour, whose husband is sick in bed.

We were almost there when we saw Father Pat's servant going into the sick man's tent. The next thing we knew, we were nearly knocked flying by a trooper on a black gelding. The broth in the kettle slopped over our legs. The trooper pulled the horse up, just in front of the tent, and he started shouting: 'Come out, you damned wretches!'

Joannes struggled out, half carrying the sick man. (I think I told you that the Priest's servant is crippled, so it was not very easy for him.)

'Hold the kettle!' Katie said to me. 'I'm going to go and get Father Pat!' And off she ran.

Constable Lord (that's the name of the trooper) demanded that the men show their licences. With his little bit of English, Joannes explained that he does not need a licence because he is the Priest's servant, and he does not dig for gold.

'*Damn you and the Priest!*' shouted Lord. He jumped off his mount and struck Joannes such a blow that the poor man fell down, and the horse began to trample him. I dumped the kettle on the ground and ran to hold the gelding's bridle. (I am not at all afraid of horses any more.)

By now there was quite a crowd gathered around, crying '*Shame!*' Up rode another official from the Camp. (This one had lots of gold braid on his uniform. I later found out that he was Assistant Commissioner Johnston.) Of course, everyone thought he would arrest Trooper Lord for assaulting poor Joannes.

It was at this point that Katie arrived back, with Father Pat. He explained that Joannes is his servant, and reminded the officials that there is a special law that says Priests and their servants do not have to have licences. But the Assistant Commissioner simply would not listen, and Father Pat had to give him five pounds bail money for Joannes Gregorius.

By the time the excitement was over, it was too late to go back to school, so Katie and I practised our parts all afternoon. I think the play will work well.

Wednesday 11 October 1854
Weather: still very hot and windy

Practised the play again with Katie at dinnertime. Now Maeve and Colleen want to be in it too. But there aren't any parts for them. They said they could be Judith's sisters, and help her kill the wicked king. I told them that didn't happen, and we cannot change History. The wind was making me feel hot and strange.

Katie suggested we go and ask Father Pat, because he is our Patron, but when we got there, he was talking to Danny Hayes's father. There was another man there too, whom Katie said is called Mr Lalor. (He lives near Katie's family, so she knows him quite well. He is tall, with a square sort of face and a bushy beard. He would be quite a few years younger than Mr Flanagan, but Katie says that all the men on the Eureka field respect him.)

Anyway, all three of them were very cross about what happened at this morning's Court case. First of all Joannes Gregorius was fined for not having a licence. So Father Pat's five pounds bail money turned into the fine. And then the Magistrate called Joannes back and dropped the charge, because he suddenly agreed that the law says that a Priest's servant does not need to have a licence. So Father Pat got his money back. The next minute, Joannes was charged with assaulting Constable Lord. And the Priest had to pay over the five pounds again!

'It is not so much the money!' Father Pat kept saying. 'It is the principle of the thing. Poor Joannes is the victim, not the perpetrator!'

I do not exactly know what a perpetrator is (unless it is like a traitor), but it is true that Joannes was the victim. His face is cut and bruised, and he is limping even more than usual. Danny's father and Mr Lalor are going to organise a petition for all the Catholics to sign, saying they don't think the Court was fair.

Anyway, Katie and I did not think it was a good time to talk about the play with our Patron.

'*Heus!*' we exclaimed. '*Eamus ad Latibulum!*' *

It was too hot to pan for *aurum*, so we took our petticoats off and sat in the *aqua frigida* of the *flumen*. After we had been there a while and had cooled off, I said that Maeve and Colleen could be Judith's maid's sisters.

Another licence hunt was going on as we came home. They happen about every second day now.

* I will translate for you, Jennychen: 'Ho! Let's go to the Hiding Place!'

Thursday 12 October 1854
Weather: hot and windy

Wrote in good new parts for the maid's sisters—helping carry the basket with the head in it, washing blood off the dagger, and so on. Maeve and Colleen very ungrateful. They complain that they want to say lines. I know that they would only forget them. And there is nothing for them to say.

Feel out of sorts with the hot northerly. It blows all the dust around. Mama is feeling it badly too. She finds it difficult to bend over the campfire and cook in this heat. The baby will be here by the end of the year, she says. I hope, if it is a sister, she is not as difficult as Maeve or Colleen.

Katie seems cross with me as well. I do not know why. I have been trying to do this play for so long, and it seems destined never to work out. (I wonder if you and Laura have yet performed it. I cannot wait for your next letter, Jennychen. I wish Europe were closer, and the boats did not take so long to go back and forth.)

All the adults are cross too. There was an Inquiry this morning into the murder. Mr Bentley went before the Magistrate and the Commissioner for the Ballarat Goldfield (who is called Mr Rede). But nothing happened. Everyone says the Magistrate is a good friend of Bentley's and secretly owns part of the Eureka Hotel.

It seems very unfair that the Magistrate was so nasty to poor Joannes Gregorius yesterday and made Father Pat pay five pounds, and today Mr Bentley does not even get charged with murder. (He is back at the Eureka Hotel now. That is where all the police and soldiers and Camp officials drink. If you walk down the road, you can hear them celebrating.)

Mama is complaining because she bought a quarter of mutton half an hour ago and already it is flyblown and crawling with maggots. The men wear veils hanging down from their hats now, to keep the flies off.

Saturday 14 October 1854

The Flanagans have appealed to our Patron. This morning Maeve and Colleen stayed back with Katie after Catechism. I arrived just expecting to have a Latin lesson, but Katie had arranged with Father Pat that we would rehearse the play in front of him, and he would advise us what to do.

So we did the play in the Chapel, with Joannes Gregorius as the audience. (Father Pat read the part of Holofernes, because Raffy was working of course.) I thought it went really well (except that Maeve and Colleen get in the way). But can you imagine what Father Pat said? He thought that Katie would be better as Judith, and I should be the maid.

'But it is my play!' I wanted to say that, but I didn't. Actually, I didn't say anything because I felt as if I might cry, if I tried to speak.

I was so upset that when it was time for the Latin lesson I got mixed up and said my verb conjugations wrong, and Katie was better than me at Latin too.

Afterwards I told her I had to help Mama and I couldn't go to the *Latibulum* today. I bet she'll find a nugget of *aurum* without me, but I do not give a *ficus*. (That means 'a fig'.)

I still like Father Pat, but I know he is wrong about the play. How could someone with hair the colour of a carrot be Judith, who was Jewish, and had black hair like mine? I will appeal to Raffy tomorrow, when Katie and I go for our Italian lesson.

Later

Mr Lalor has just arrived at our camp. I thought he must be bringing the petition about what happened to Joannes Gregorius. (I have seen Danny's father taking it around the Eureka field, for people to sign.) But it turns out that he wants Mama to mend a couple of shirts for him. (He does not have a wife.) That's good. Mr Lalor has a lot of mates, and if he gets them all to bring their sewing to Mama, then she won't worry so much about money.

(My boots get tighter and tighter. When I go to the bush with Katie I take them off and walk barefoot. The soles of my feet are becoming leathery, like the nuts around the gum flowers.)

Sunday 15 October 1854

The last Mass bell has rung and now I would usually run down and meet Katie. But I have decided to revise my Italian vocabulary before our lesson this afternoon. (Do not want to let Katie be better at that as well as Latin.)

It looks as if they are holding a meeting now outside the Chapel. There are even more men there than usual. I suppose it is about what happened to poor Joannes Gregorius. Some people call the diggers on Eureka 'the Tipperary Mob', because they are nearly all Irish.

Monday 16 October 1854

School was abominable this afternoon. I finished embroidering my passage onto my sampler (I did all the writing in red, for the robin redbreast) and I took it up to show Mrs Cadwallader and she said I *have* to unpick it all because it is not neat enough and besides, she says I have to put something from the Bible onto it. So I sat there unpicking all my weeks of work. I have decided that I am not going to go to school tomorrow. What is the point when they just make me undo work I have done? I would do better to stay home!

(Except of course I cannot stay home or Mama will know that I am wagging. I will pretend to go, and then go and hide at the Hidden Valley.)

Came straight home after school this afternoon. I do not feel like practising the play. Yesterday afternoon Raffy listened to Katie and me do the parts, and he agreed that Katie would be a better Judith. He said she could wear a shawl to cover her hair. The maid does not do anything interesting. And now I have given her two stupid sisters!

Today four men wearing sou'wester hats and black veils held up the Bank of Victoria (on Sturt Street, near the Government Camp) and stole fifteen thousand pounds. Then they made their escape. All the adults are asking what is the point of paying their licence fees to support the police force when the police cannot even protect the gold in the bank?

To add insult to injury, there is a licence hunt going on now. One good thing about having so many of them is that Mama does not even seem to notice them anymore.

Have to go and get Tulip soon. The men are working longer hours now. Vati is determined that they will bottom soon. (They have been getting occasional little bits of gold from the washdirt, but when it is divided four ways, there is not much. Katie did not go to the Hidden Valley on Saturday, so she did not find nuggets without me. That is one good thing at least.)

I can see Danny Hayes and some of the other boys nailing notices onto trees. Something must be happening!

Tuesday 17 October 1854
Weather: another hot nasty northerly wind

Dawn

It is very strange. My father has said that I need not get Tulip today. It seems that everybody has decided to have a holiday. (If some diggers do not work their claim, then everybody has to stop, or the water rises in the shafts. Do not ask me why! But that is why they all work or they all rest at the same time.)

But although they are not going to work, the diggers are not lazing in their tents as they do on Sundays. They are grabbing a bit of damper from last night and hurrying off without their proper breakfasts.

I'll follow before Mama can stop me.

Later

Such excitement!

There was a huge meeting this morning at the place where poor Mr Scobie was murdered. (That's what the notices on the trees were about. The ones Danny and his friends were nailing up yesterday.)

I had to be careful that my father did not see me, but Katie and I managed to wriggle close to the front. We watched as various men took turns to get up on the stump and speak. They were saying that the Inquiry into the death of Mr Scobie was a sham, and they were complaining because the police have done nothing to find the murderer. (Everybody still thinks that Bentley did it.) One of the speakers was my rescuer in the red sash. (Katie says that people call him Captain Ross, though she does not know why he is a Captain. She agrees he is very handsome.)

After a while, the diggers voted to raise money for a Reward for anyone who gives evidence that gets the murderer convicted. Mr Lalor was put in charge of collecting the money. (He was wearing one of the shirts that Mama mended for him.)

By that time my legs were tired and it looked like the talking was going to go on for ever, so Katie and Maeve and Colleen and I went back to the Flanagans' tent and started to practise the play. Katie is now the heroine of course, but the story is changing a bit, so that the maid and her sisters and Judith go together to kill the wicked tyrant King.

I was so busy writing in new lines that I forgot all about the meeting. And then we heard so much noise that we ran out. By this time the sun was high in the sky (and very hot), and a huge crowd was gathered outside the Eureka Hotel. (Vati later said there were ten thousand people there.) I think quite a lot of the diggers had been drinking nobblers. There were also policemen there on horses.

The next thing we saw, a man came out of the Hotel and rode away fast on a horse, towards the Government Camp. Someone shouted that it was Bentley. By now all the diggers had got very cross.

Some of Danny's friends were there, and they started throwing stones at the Hotel, just for fun, and one of them broke the glass lamp outside the front door. Katie and I heard the glass break.

It was as if it was a signal. Within seconds, men as well as boys were throwing stones at the Eureka Hotel, and the windows were smashing, and then men were ripping boards off the building, and suddenly a whole troop of soldiers marched up, and stood in a line in front of the Hotel. Commissioner Rede climbed up onto a window sill and started talking, but no-one could hear him. Some people threw rubbish and rotten eggs at him.

How did the fire start? Nobody seems to know. But suddenly the Bowling Alley beside the Hotel was alight. As the gusty wind fanned the flames, the fire jumped from the canvas walls of the Bowling Saloon to the wooden boards of the Hotel.

You would have expected the soldiers to try to stop the fire, but they just formed ranks and marched back to the Camp! Within a minute or two, the building was a blazing inferno.

Meanwhile all the diggers in the crowd were laughing, and enjoying watching the fire. Soon Mr Bentley's Hotel was burned right to the ground, and all that was left was smoking rubble and mounds of broken glass.

Katie nudged me. '*Fervida sum*,' she said. 'Let us go to the *aqua frigida*.'

Instantly her little sisters' ears were flapping.

'Where are you going?

'Can we come?'

'What are you saying?'

'It's not fair!'

'*Secretum!*' I warned Katie.

And we ran through the tents of the Eureka field, towards the bush. By the time we reached the first line of wattle trees, we had left the little girls behind. Soon we were in the Hidden Valley, cooling off in the creek. I feel so happy to be friends with Katie again that I do not really mind if she is Judith. Raffy told me that people who are very good writers are often not very good actors. (I hope he is a good actor, because of course he is going to be our wicked King.)

There was an amazing hailstorm as we came back from the creek. Then rain. I feel as if my crossness and strangeness of the last few days has been washed away.

Wednesday 18 October 1854

When I came out from school at dinnertime, the Tipperary mob was meeting again outside the Chapel. All the Catholics are still very angry about poor Joannes's injury and Father Pat's five pounds. Saw Katie and Maeve and Colleen at the meeting, so we started saying our lines for the play. Danny and the other boys were watching us, and now they want to be in it. They say they would be better at killing the King. Katie and I said: 'NO!'

Thursday 19 October 1854
Weather: hot and dusty

I am in the most terrible trouble. My parents have discovered that I wagged school on Tuesday. Mama is cross because she has been mending shirts to pay my one shilling and sixpence school fees every week. Vati is cross because I am missing out on my education. Actually Vati is cross all the time, because he cannot find any gold. And because of what is happening with the police and the Court and everything. (About fifty more police arrived from Melbourne today—mostly horse police, but some on foot as well.) But now Vati is cross at me as well. I think he should stay home and teach me himself, like he used to do. He never got cross at me in those days.

As a punishment I have to stay here on Saturday and help Mama, instead of going to the *Latibulum* with Katie. If my parents would only let me go and find some *aurum*, then they would not have to be cross about money.

Saturday 21 October 1854

Punishment day! Mama has warned me that when I come back from my Latin lesson I will have lanterns and kettles to clean, and kindling to fetch.

Later

There is much excitement at the moment because the news is going around that the police have arrested two men for being ringleaders in the hotel fire.

Men are already stopping work (you can hear the

silence as the cradles stop rocking and the windlasses stop cranking up and down) and I can see a great number of people walking up to Bakery Hill. (That is the highest point in this part of Ballarat. If you stand on top of it you can look right across to the Government Camp and see the soldiers marching around the Union Jack on its pole at the centre of the parade ground.)

Haec scribens interpellata sum! Katie has just arrived to help me with my jobs.

Later still

Katie has gone home again now.

The meeting has finished and a great many men are marching down the Main Road now, shouting and cheering and firing off their revolvers into the air. Mama is anxious in case any bullets go astray, but Vati says the diggers are just excited because they have joined together to find five hundred pounds to bail out the two prisoners. My father says that that is five times more than the bail money for Mr Bentley.

Monday 23 October 1854

I was GOING to go back to school this afternoon. I really was. I went this morning. That was bad enough. Sitting there so bored as we read the *Fourth Book* around the class. As the dinner bell rang, Mrs Cadwallader reminded me that I would need to choose a passage to sew on my sampler this afternoon. She even lent me a Bible to bring home. And I really was going to go back and do my Needlework. But first I went to Katie's camp to practise the play. Did I tell you that Danny and the other boys are in it now? But it is still Judith (Katie) and her best friend (me) who lead the Rebellion against the King.

And then, instead of doing the play, Katie and I helped Danny go around the Eureka field reminding everyone about the meeting. (There were already notices on tree stumps, that the boys stuck up yesterday.) It was such a lark! We had goldmining pans and tin spoons, and we went around like a band, yelling out and drumming.

'COME TO THE MEETING! BAKERY HILL! TWO O'CLOCK!'

And of course I ended up in the procession of diggers walking up there at the end of dinnertime. (People say that once again there were ten thousand there.) And somehow I didn't quite get back to school.

Mr Humffray spoke at the meeting, and the other men whom my father calls 'the Chartists'. Everybody decided to form a Diggers' Rights Society. Then my father saw me! I thought he was going to explode on the spot. It is all very well for him and his mates to talk about FREEDOM and RIGHTS, but what about MY right not to be persecuted by Mrs Cadwallader, and bored to death by the *Fourth Book?* That's what I started to say.

'And where are your boots?' my father interrupted.

'I left them at Katie's tent,' I told him, but did not tell him why. I mostly do not wear them anymore, even around the diggings.

'Well make sure Katie brings them back,' he said as he sent me home.

Which is where I am now. Writing this. Mama is not here but when Vati comes back I will be in such trouble about school again. I fear that my parents may stop me from seeing Katie and practising the play.

Later

It is strange, what has happened. Just after my father got home (still looking like thunder), Katie arrived with my boots. She also brought Mrs Cadwallader's Bible, which I had left at her tent at dinnertime. Vati wanted to know what I was doing with it, and then the whole story came out, about the sampler, and how I was not allowed to embroider 'All Power Proceeds from the People', and then how I was forced to unpick what William Blake said about the robin redbreast, and how I HAVE to embroider a Bible passage. And my father stopped being angry with me, and he started being really, really angry with Mrs Cadwallader—and he has said that I do not have to go to school anymore.

Hurray!

. . . Mama just came home. She had been at the Government Camp, fitting Mrs Beaumont for a tea-gown. She reports that the ladies are very frightened, because there are only four hundred and fifty soldiers and police there, and they fear that the diggers will attack and overpower them! How silly they are.

Wednesday 25 October 1854

Now that I do not go to school, I have to help Mama more. But I do not mind. Katie and her sisters and I have a sort of sledge that we can pull along, and we go out collecting kindling. Or if Tulip is not needed at the mine, we harness it behind her and collect big pieces of firewood. We keep our eyes peeled for gold, wherever we go. (Sometimes when we go into the bush we see poor Mrs Tredinnick gathering wattle. People say she puts a fresh bunch every day on her husband's grave. It is sad like a romantic novel, isn't it, Jennychen?)

More soldiers from the 40th Regiment arrived today. Mama is busy taking orders for gowns, because the ladies hope to have a ball in the new Arcade. She sent me up to the Camp today to ask 'Does Mrs Thomas want the small pearl buttons or the medium?' Some of the ladies are moving out of the Camp and into the Hotels in the main part of Town. People are saying that Something is going to happen tomorrow, but nobody knows what it may be.

My father does not like Mama to be sewing for the Camp ladies, but at the moment that is the only money we can get. I am determined that Katie and I will strike gold and save our parents from disaster!

Thursday 26 October 1854

Today Mama wanted me to take a message to town, for a lady called Mrs Henry Seekamp. (Mr Seekamp has started coming to Vati's reading group. He is the editor of the *Ballarat Times*.) When I got to the address, you would never guess who opened the door! Yes—it was none other than Lady Macbeth. Who of course is Miss Clara du Val. Who turns out to be married to Mr Seekamp. She is SO beautiful, and her voice is deep and sort of echoes. I was too shy to say anything, and just gave her the note. (Mama is mending one of her gowns.) But next time I am determined to speak to her. If I am especially brave I might invite her to come and see our play.

Oh, and the Thing that everybody was wondering about happened at first light this morning. The police and soldiers rode out, and arrested ten more men for the fire at Mr Bentley's Hotel.

All the adults are cross about it, but the men are

still working and there isn't a meeting like there was on Saturday when the first two men were arrested.

Wednesday 1 November 1854

Rehearsals are postponed because Danny and his mates and Katie and I have been gathering lots and lots of firewood. We are going to have the biggest bonfire on Guy Fawkes night! (That is upside down here too of course. It is hot work to be getting wood in summertime.)

Raffy gave us some moth-holey trousers and a dreadful old coat, and Katie and I have stuffed them with newspapers and made a Guy to put on the fire. We have painted a face onto his rag-head, and he has a beautiful blue hat with white cockatoo feathers and gold braid (painted on) for he is also to be Governor Hotham. (Raffy suggested his identity.) There is to be a meeting at Bakery Hill this afternoon, so Danny and Katie and I are going to take our Guy along and ask people for money. This is our song:

> *Remember, remember*
> *The fifth of November,*
> *Gunpowder, treason and plot.*
> *The King and his train*
> *Had like to be slain*
> *And we hope it will ne'er be forgot.*

We hope to get a lot of money because all the diggers hate the Governor now, and they will be happy to think of him burning on our fire. The money is to buy material for the costumes we need for the circus. We have decided on blue cloaks, like the ones that Mrs Rowe's Equestrians had, so that we shall look splendid as we ride out and do our tricks. The cloaks will cover our play costumes, for of course we shall not be able to get changed between the first circus act and the beginning of the play.

Later

Today's meeting was not so large as usual—only three thousand people—but we managed to collect quite a lot of pennies for our Guy. (We spent some on lemonade, for Mr Thonen was there with his cart. And we went to the lolly shop too.)

My father was at the meeting of course, but this time he did not mind me being there. He liked our Guy, but he said we should sing 'Gunpowder *reason*' instead of 'treason' because if Mr Guy Fawkes and his friends had succeeded in blowing up the British Parliament, then we might have a Republic.

Saw my friend and rescuer, Captain Ross, and he gave every single one of us a penny for our Guy! (With Danny's friends, that came to over a shilling.) Captain

Ross also made a speech from the stump. He is in charge of making sure that the men arrested for the fire are properly defended in Court.

Most of the speeches were about how the diggers want to have the vote, so they can choose people to represent them in the Victorian Parliament. My father says it is unfair that they have to pay the Governor a lot of money for the licence fees, but they do not have any power over how that money is spent.

Anyway, when all the yabber yabber finished, there was a parade of bands and banners down the Main Road. Groups of diggers from different countries carried their national flags—German, French, Welsh, Mexican, American, Polish, Irish and so on. Danny and the other boys and Katie and Maeve and Colleen and I walked along at the end with Governor Hotham (we had his name on a sign, pinned onto his breast) and a lot of the diggers laughed and cheered and threw pennies. Some even fired off their revolvers into the air, like firecrackers.

I know we are going to have a wonderful bonfire on Sunday night, and we will raise enough money to buy our blue cloaks.

Monday 6 November 1854

Wouldn't you know it? It started raining when Katie and I were at Raffy's for Italian yesterday afternoon, and it rained and it rained and it rained, so that by dusk we all knew that there was no hope of having our bonfire. We have decided to wait now until next Saturday night, for there is to be another Monster Meeting that afternoon, and we might as well take Governor Hotham along and get some more pennies.

Sun is shining now, and soon Mama and I will set off for the creek with the hamper of dirty clothes. (Mama does most of the washing for J J and Alphonse and Sancho Panza, as well as for our own little family.)

Monday is wash day for all the women of the diggings, and the creek bank is always dotted with fires boiling up big cauldrons of water for soaking, and kettles of water for tea. Meanwhile the women and children sit at the water's edge, scrubbing the clothes on washboards. (Mind you, the water is so muddy from the men puddling in it that Mama sometimes says that clothes come out dirtier than they went in.) Katie's mother helps Mama, for she is so large now that she finds it hard to bend over the washboard. When the clothes are done, we hang them on the bushes. Then it is time for a cup of tea, and all the women talk and joke together, while they wait for the washing to dry.

Mama always comes home really happy after wash days.

Sunday 12 November 1854

Am writing this while Katie is at Mass.

Yesterday was a great success. There were thousands and thousands of people at Bakery Hill, and we took Governor Hotham's hat off and used it to collect money in. (We'd put him on the sledge and we all took turns dragging him around behind us.) By the end of the afternoon the hat was filled up with pennies and halfpennies—and even a few threepences and sixpences. We will have enough money to buy the material for our costumes, and Mama has promised to help make them. (But she says that I have to do some sewing on them too.)

The meeting was a lot of adult yabber yabber while they decided the charter of the Ballarat Reform League. (My father thinks it is so important that he is writing to your father about it at this very minute. Hurray! It means I will be able to send the next instalment of this journal-letter off to you tomorrow.) The League is not just about the licence fees and the hunts, but about being allowed to vote and be represented in Parliament and have a Democracy.

When all the men were cheering about the demand for Manhood Suffrage, Miss du Val called out that there should be Suffrage for Women too. Did I tell you that she has become our co-Patron? She has promised to hear Katie and me go through our parts, and give us advice about Voice Projection. We have agreed that Danny and the other boys can be in the play (as well as doing circus acts at the beginning). But of course Katie and I still have the main roles.

The story has changed a bit now, and it is about a whole lot of people who rise up against a wicked tyrant King who oppresses them with heavy taxes and does not let them vote in the Government. While the heroine and her maid assassinate the King, the Conspirators (Danny and his friends) blow up the Parliament. Then there is a Republic. Raffy says that the play is sure to be very popular around the diggings, and lots of people will want to buy tickets. We have chosen the first Sunday in December as the date for our Grande Performance. (As long as the weather is good.)

Had our Guy Fawkes bonfire last night, after the meeting was over. We have been dragging poor old Governor Hotham around for so long that I was almost sorry to see him burn. When the flames died down, we roasted potatoes in the coals.

Monday 20 November 1854

Vati's reading group is meeting as I write this. The weather is so warm now that they no longer sit around the fire, but have the logs arranged in a big circle between the tents. Mr Seekamp is here tonight, as well as Mr Humffray and both Mr Blacks, plus Mr Lalor and Raffy and the lemonade man and Mr Joseph and a few others who always come. These days Vati sometimes writes a little article for Mr Seekamp's newspaper, but he doesn't have much time. (He tries to spend Sunday making notes for his guidebook about How To Be a Successful Gold Digger in the Colony of Victoria. Mama sometimes says he does not seem to know very much about his topic.)

. . . I wish Miss du Val would come to reading group. Katie and I had our first Voice Projection lesson with her last week. We are doing this new thing now in the play where I am the narrator, and I stand out the front and set the scene and tell the audience where we are and what happens in between scenes. That is useful, because we cannot have scenery or curtains as we will be performing outdoors. There is a fairly flat bit of land down near where Katie lives, and we have decided to use that as our performing space. Because of the horses, we need quite a lot of room. It is hard to find level, open land in Ballarat for there are mine shafts and mounds of earth everywhere, and it is dangerous to bring horses over most of the diggings because of all the holes. That is why the troopers do not ride in among the mines and tents in the licence hunts. So this is really the best place we can find. And as it is close to the Flanagans' tent, we can store the costumes and props there.

. . . *Haec scribens interpellata sum.* Mama needed me to take the kettle of tea around, and pour it into the men's pannikins.

Vati and the men were all saying how they wonder what happened in Melbourne today. (It takes a couple of days before the newspapers arrive here.) They were all talking about the Trial. At first I thought they meant of the murderer, Mr Bentley. (He was found guilty of Manslaughter before the Melbourne Court last Friday, but he only has to go to gaol for three years.) But there was another Trial there today, of the three men who are being blamed for lighting the fire at the Eureka Hotel. The other men who were arrested were all let off, and everyone is saying it is unfair that these three men are being blamed, because *no-one* could say *who* started the fire. There were so many thousands of people there, the police might as well arrest everyone. Including me and Katie! And especially Danny's friends, because they were the ones who started breaking the windows of the Hotel. So to choose three people out of a whole crowd is like when Mrs Cadwallader used to pick on Katie and blame her for talking in class and keep her in, when it was everyone who was talking (except for me, because no-one would talk to me).

Wednesday 22 November 1854
Weather: hot and sticky like a date pudding

Mama had to go to Town today to buy some lining silk, so Katie and I took the opportunity of accompanying her, and choosing the material for our cloaks. We had all our Guy pennies tied up in a big kerchief—it was ever so heavy.

I think you would like what we have chosen. The blue is perhaps more like the ocean than the sky, or perhaps it is like the sky in the evening. Katie and I like it very well, and Mama says it will be serviceable and will not show the dirt. We bought all that was left on the bolt, as it was a little cheaper that way, but you should have seen the proprietor's face when she told us the price, and Katie opened up our bundle of coppers! The lady was counting for a full half hour, but there was enough over for us to pay a visit to the lolly shop and to buy a lemonade each from Mr Thonen.

I was eager for Mama to cut the cloth as soon as we got home, and to begin making the cloaks, but Mama says we have to wait until she is finished all the dresses she is making for her ladies, who have besieged her with work.

That is hard for her at the moment, because of her Condition, but it is lucky she is earning some money because when I met my father at the mine, he told me that they struck a shicer today.

To make matters worse, all the diggers are feeling despondent because the news arrived from Melbourne that the three men tried for the fire at Bentley's Hotel have been found Guilty, and are to go to gaol for a few months.

Oh well. I know our Grande Performance will cheer everybody up. (Only a week and a bit to go. I cannot wait!)

Friday 24 November 1854

Mama has decided to employ Mrs Flanagan to help her with tacking the linings, so Katie's mother will be spending quite a bit of time at our tent. The two mothers keep threatening Katie and me that we should be sewing as well, but so far we have managed to escape!

Saturday 25 November 1854

Dinnertime

This afternoon Katie and I plan to go to the *Latibulum* together. We have been so busy lately—organising the play, practising the circus, doing our Italian and Latin lessons, collecting firewood, running errands for Mama to Town—that we have not had any time to pan for gold.

I just feel it in my bones that we shall be lucky today.

Night-time

WE DID IT WE DID IT WE DID IT WE DID IT!!!

We did find some *aurum* today! Some beautiful golden yellow *aurum*, lying in the bottom of our dirty old *patella!* *Aurum* like Rapunzel's hair! *Aurum* like wattle! *Aurum* like money!

We squashed the little grains together and put them in a matchbox, then we buried that under the big gum tree, and put leaves down so no-one could see where we had disturbed the earth. We want to wait until we have some more before we give it to our parents.

When we came back to the creek paddocks, Danny and the boys were there, practising their circus tricks. They are getting good, I do have to say. They have even tied a washing line between two trees, and are practising walking on it. They don't fall off very often.

It was time to go and get the horses, so Katie and I did that, and then we practised our bareback riding until it was too dark to see. I find it easy now to ride standing up (as long as Tulip does not trot).

Sunday 26 November 1854

We practised the play and circus this afternoon in the actual performance space. It went very well (except that the boys take too long at the beginning with their acrobatics and juggling, which means there is less time for the equestrian acts, and Colleen still forgets her lines quite often). It is all a bit frightening, because we only have a week more practising, before the Grande Performance next Sunday afternoon. Miss Du Val came today, to watch us. She said I have a good clear voice and make an excellent narrator. I would still secretly prefer to be Judith, but I know that Katie is really really good in the role. Raffy too was very good today. He stuffed three pillows into his trousers, which makes him a wonderfully fat wicked tyrant King. When Katie plunges the dagger in, of course it just sinks in between the pillows. (It is a stage prop that Miss du Val lent us from the Gravel Pits Theatre, and is the very same dagger that she uses for Lady Macbeth, so we have to be careful not to lose it.)

Had to cut our practice a bit short because Danny's father came and asked if the boys could nail up the notices for the next meeting. (Mr Humffray and Mr Black have gone to Melbourne and are going to visit Governor Hotham tomorrow. They are going to ask him to release the three men who were put in prison for burning the Hotel. So there is going to be a meeting on Wednesday, for them to report back to the diggers what the Governor says.)

While the boys put up the notices, Katie and I gave out the handbills. I kept a spare one, so I will paste it in this journal for you ...

DOWN WITH THE LICENCE FEES!

DOWN WITH DESPOTISM!

"WHO SO BASE AS TO BE A SLAVE?"

ON

WEDNESDAY NEXT

the 29th. Instant, at Two o'clock

A MEETING

Of all the DIGGERS, STOREKEEPERS, and inhabitants of Ballarat Generally, will be held

ON BAKERY HILL

For the immediate Abolition of the Licence Fee, and the speedy attainment of the other objects of the Ballarat Reform League. The report of the Deputations which have gone to the Lieutenant-Governor to demand the release of the prisoners lately convicted, and to Creswick and Forest Creeks, Bendigo, &c., will also be submitted at the same time.
All who claim the right to a voice in the framing of the Laws under which they live, are solemnly bound to attend the Meeting and further its objects to the utmost extent of their power.

N.B. Bring your licences, they may be wanted.

Printed at the "TIMES" Office, Bakery Hill, Ballarat.

Monday 27 November 1854

Morning

Poor Mama has so many fittings to do today that we are missing out on the wash day picnic. The American Consul is holding a Reception here in Ballarat tomorrow night, to celebrate Thanksgiving Day. A number of the Government ladies have been invited, and are demanding that their new gowns be ready for the occasion. Mama wants me to hold the pins and things, so I have to accompany her up to Town. (Nearly all the ladies have left the Camp now, and live in lodging houses. The Camp is like a fort of soldiers.)

Looks like being a stinking hot day. Pardon my expression, Jennychen, but with all the livers and heads and tails and things lying around all the butchers' shambles, it really does smell here sometimes. And poor Mama is finding the heat so very hard to bear.

Evening
Katie had to look after Tulip for me, as I am only now back from Town. Mama did the fitting and finishing on no less than a dozen gowns today, and she has eight more to do tomorrow. I feel as if I shall scream, if I ever see another pin! Or perhaps I would just stab it into the nearest lady.

They treat my mother and me like servants, Jennychen, and expect Mama to work all day without a break, although her Condition is very noticeable. And then they keep her waiting weeks for her money, although the diggers always pay on the spot when she mends a shirt. (My father says that the rich never pay, and that is how they become rich.) But most insulting of all is the way that the ladies gossip in front of us, as if we were not even there. Most of the conversation is just mushy romantic talk about various officers, but a few of them were also saying that they hope the attack does not come tomorrow night, and spoil the Reception.

What attack? I wondered. And then I realised that the ladies still believe that the diggers are going to rise up and attack the Camp. Mrs Thomas (the wife of Captain Thomas, who is in charge of all the soldiers) told them that Commissioner Rede fears that it will happen on Wednesday, after the meeting at Bakery Hill.

What a laugh. If there were any such plan, I would know, for Vati's friends are gathered here tonight for reading group (except for Mr Humffray and the other members of the Delegation, who are not back yet from Melbourne), and no-one is speaking of any kind of attack.

Captain Ross is just complaining about the way most of the diggers still think of themselves in their national groups, as Germans, or Irish, or Americans or whatever. 'Look at the way they wave their national flags at every opportunity!' he exclaims.

I am thinking that instead of naming all the different countries that our performers come from, we should just call ourselves 'The *United* Theatrical and Equestrian Circus Company'. I think that sounds good. Will talk to Katie about it tomorrow.

Tuesday 28 November 1854

Morning

Mama is taking Mrs Flanagan to Town to help her with the gowns today, so I do not have to go. Hurray!

Nearly Dusk

Feel very out of sorts! Honestly, Jennychen, I do not know WHY we allowed Danny and the other boys to join our play. We were meant to be having our first full rehearsal this afternoon. (Without the cloaks, of course. Mama however promises that as soon as the silly ladies' silly Reception is over, then she shall make our costumes.) But we got nothing done at rehearsal for, no sooner would we start to go through our parts, than the boys would run off to count the soldiers who kept arriving along the roads from Geelong and Creswick and Melbourne. (Indeed, I think that—as well as counting—the boys were hooting and shouting, and some later boasted that they had thrown stones.) All in all, they say, two hundred and forty-six more soldiers arrived at the Camp today and thirty-nine mounted police. You would think that boys would grow sick of looking at soldiers. (Katie and I do not give two figs how many redcoats we see. Oh! And Katie agrees about the new name for our Company.)

I can see Captain Ross coming towards our tent. I suppose he is looking for Vati, but the men are not here yet.

Later

What a surprise, Jennychen! It was not my father but my mother whom the Canadian was coming to see. He began in that polite way of his—taking his hat off and bowing. 'I was wondering if I could bother you, Ma'am, to help me out with a spot of needlework . . .'

I naturally thought that he had a shirt that needed mending, or perhaps some trousers that had become ripped, so I was not really paying attention. And then I realised that the Captain was asking my mother to make a new flag, to fly from Bakery Hill at tomorrow's meeting. 'We need some sort of symbol that will unite everyone,' he said. 'No matter what country they come from.'

I felt really proud of my mother, that the Captain should ask her. It is proof that everyone acknowledges she is the finest seamstress in Ballarat.

However Mama did not seem at all delighted to be chosen. She simply replied: 'You know, sir, that I would do anything within my power to help you.' (She was referring to her promise, after the Captain saved my life.)

'Even if there were some danger involved?' asked the Captain.

My mother nodded. For Mama, a promise is a promise, and must be kept.

But how can a flag be dangerous? I wondered. Mama and I made the gold and scarlet flag to fly from our tent pole when first we arrived here. It is still flying—and has never caused any danger. I do not understand.

'And what do you want it to look like?' my mother asked. 'This new flag that will include all the people?'

Captain Ross seemed embarrassed. 'I thought you might have some ideas . . .'

My mother shrugged, as if to say: 'Well, that is the end of that!'

And then suddenly I thought of something. '*We could put the Southern Cross on it!*' I told them. '*That shines upon us all, no matter who we are or where we come from.*'

My mother looked at me, and I knew that I had won her over. Quickly she took a stick and drew a rectangle in the sandy soil. Inside that she made lines, to form a cross. At the four points and in the centre she sketched a star. Like this, Jennychen:

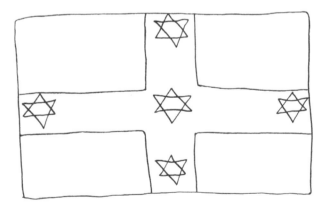

'Deep blue for the sky,' Mama said firmly, 'with a white cross and stars. Will that suit you, Captain?'

'Perfect!' Captain Ross tipped his hat. 'I thank you, Ma'am. I shall pay for the cloth, of course.'

As he walked away, my mother muttered: 'Typical man! He does not even wonder where we shall get the material at this time of the evening. The shops must be nearly closing!'

'Will you be able to do it in time?' I asked.

'With a little bit of help,' Mama said. She suddenly looked at me very seriously. 'You must run down and ask Katie's mother and Danny's mother to come. The girls may come too. But you must not tell anybody else.'

'Is it a secret?'

'A very big secret,' my mother told me.

SO! That was over an hour ago. Mrs Flanagan and Mrs Hayes came back to our tent, where they are talking now. Katie and her sisters have been sent to Town to buy the cloth. They should have been back by now . . .

Something is happening! I can hear bullets going off, and the sound of shouting, and people are running down towards the Eureka field. I hope that Katie is safe.

. . . Everyone is saying that there has been an ambush. An escort of soldiers was coming up the Melbourne road, bringing new supplies of guns and ammunition, and as they marched past the Eureka field, a group of diggers leaped out of the darkness and held the escort up. The diggers just wanted to take the guns, so they couldn't be used against the people, but there was a terrible accident, and the drummer boy has been killed. And now there are soldiers riding out from the Camp . . .

Here is Katie back. So I will put this away.

Wednesday 29 November 1854

Very early in the morning

What a strange night it has been. And the strangeness is still happening. I am lying on my little cot, Jennychen, and around me there is the soft light thrown by the lamp, and across the canvas are the shadows of the women who sit in our tent, making the flag. I feel as I am dreaming and have entered a magical world, and I should pinch myself to be sure I am real. Earlier tonight, when Katie and her sisters and I were helping stitch the flag, Mama said that we girls must remember this night for as long as we live. That is why I am writing it down for you, Jennychen, so that you can remind me if I ever forget . . .

Perhaps I should begin with the cloth. I am sure that you have already realised how we got the blue for the sky. Yes, we let Mama use the circus cloak material. I knew that we should have to, when Katie came back from her errand, saying that the stores were already shut, and there was no material to be bought. But I felt cross at first, for I hate the way that adults think that their concerns are more important than what children are doing.

'You can help us make the flag,' Mama told me, as if that were any consolation.

Why would I want to sew a stupid old flag?

'Yes, girls,' said Katie's ma. 'This will be something to tell your grandchildren about!'

Who wants grandchildren? I thought.

Already I could see Mama slashing through the blue material with her scissors, to make four large rectangles.

Slash slash slash slash. Goodbye circus costumes!

I thought of us riding around the ring without our cloaks, and I felt a lump swell up in my throat. It wasn't fair!

'Go and throw some tea-leaves in the kettle,' Mrs Flanagan told Katie and me. 'We could all do with a drop.'

So we went out to the fire. My father and all the other men have gone off somewhere, so it was strangely quiet around the camp site. And then I saw a shadow move in the darkness. I jumped, thinking it was perhaps a trooper, or maybe one of the police spies that are around. (Mama had explained to me that if the Government found out that a diggers' flag was being made, they would want to stop it, and might even arrest whoever was involved. That was what Captain Ross had meant about the danger.)

As the shadow moved, I wished I had Bonaparte here, to frighten the stranger off. And then I saw that it was Mrs Tredinnick, whom I sometimes see picking wattle. She was standing there in her dark mourning dress, saying nothing, and in her arms she held a white bundle that she was cradling so carefully that for a moment I thought it was a baby.

'Our mothers are inside,' Katie said to her, as if to invite her to join the other women.

But Mrs Tredinnick thrust the bundle into my arms. 'It were our marriage sheet,' she said. 'That I used to wrap him in.' And her dark figure disappeared back into the night.

Perhaps you might think I felt squeamish, Jennychen, holding the shroud that had wrapped poor Mr Tredinnick when he was dead, but I just felt mean, that I had cared so much about our circus costumes.

So we took the tea in, and the white sheeting, which Mama cut to make the four white arms of the cross.

'It would be nice to have something transparent, for the stars,' she said. 'To let the light shine through . . .'

Do you believe in magic, Jennychen? Well, before Katie had finished pouring the pannikins of tea, the flap of the tent opened, and in stepped Miss Du Val. In her emerald silk gown, she looked far more splendid than any of the ladies from the Government Camp. 'I am no use with a needle,' she announced, 'but if I can help in any other way . . .'

I do not know why I said it, but I did. 'We need five stars,' I told her, as if she should happen to carry such things about with her.

Lo and behold, Miss du Val lifted up her skirt, and stepped out of her petticoat. 'It was clean on this evening,' she murmured as she handed the fine lawn to my mother.

Snip snip.

Stitch and stitch.

And so the minutes ticked by, as the soft folds of the banner passed from hand to hand.

If Mrs Cadwallader could see me now! That is what I thought, as I made my own little line of needlework. And then I passed my piece of blue to Katie, who hemmed on along the line.

Well, that was some hours before I started writing this to you, Jennychen, and another hour has gone by, so that now I can hear the sounds of the first birds waking up outside. Across the tent I can hear my mother and Mrs Tredinnick quietly talking as they put the finishing stitches in the stars. I have never stayed up all night until dawn before!

Late afternoon

I fell asleep this morning, just after I wrote that, and when I woke the tent was silent, and there was not so much as a pin or a piece of cotton on the earthen floor to show what went on here last night. I might have thought that I had dreamed it all, except that I could remember the feel of the silky blue sky as I pushed the needle through and made my little stitches.

But where is the flag? I panicked as I woke. And where is my mother? Where are all the other women, who came during the night and sewed for a while, before slipping away again? Did the spies find out what they were doing, and send the soldiers to arrest them all? But if so—why have I heard nothing?

I pulled on my dress and ran outside, to find the fire died down and no sign of anyone. I could tell by the sun that the time was moving towards midday.

And then I saw them walking up from the Eureka field—my mother, and Danny's mother, and Katie's mother, and the other women who helped make the flag, including Miss du Val, and poor Mrs Tredinnick. And Katie was there too, and her sisters, and between them they were carrying a laundry hamper.

Is everyone going to the creek? I wondered. *Is there washing to be done?*

But when I ran to join them, Katie opened the lid of the hamper—and I saw the folds of blue sky, and the shine of the silver stars, and then I helped Katie carry the banner in its secret hiding place all the way to Bakery Hill.

There Captain Ross and Mr Hayes and my father and Mr Seekamp and some of the other men were hammering away at a wooden platform, next to a flagpole made from the tallest and straightest tree that you have ever seen. And from the top there hung down a double line of rope.

It sounds strange, but I felt really shy, as Katie and I held out the washing basket to Captain Ross, and he took from it the folded flag, and tied the rope to the wooden toggles at top and bottom.

The men and women stood around in a small circle—there were maybe a couple of dozen there—and watched as the Captain showed Katie and me how to pull the ropes to make the flag climb slowly up the pole. As it caught for a moment, my heart caught with it, and then we pulled gently, and up it leaped to the very top. And as the breeze caught the cloth, and the Southern Cross unfurled against the sky, I thought that I would burst with pride. Some of my stitches were up there!

The meeting happened at the end of dinnertime, and my father says there were fifteen thousand there. Father Pat was on the platform, as well as Mr Lalor and

Mr Hayes. All the diggers were cross when Mr Humffray reported that Governor Hotham would not agree to release the three men who have been jailed for the Hotel fire.

And then Katie and I became cross, when Mr Lalor got everyone to agree to have another meeting next Sunday at 2 o'clock at the Adelphi Theatre, to elect a new committee for the Reform League. We had been planning to start the circus at 3 o'clock. But Miss du Val said we could change our time to 5 o'clock, and people will come after the meeting. There will still be plenty of daylight.

Raffy got up to speak too, and he called on everybody, no matter what their nationality, religion or colour, to salute the Southern Cross. He called it 'the refuge of all the oppressed people from all the countries on this earth'. Everybody cheered and cheered and cheered, and I held Mama's hand tight, and thought about that night on the ship when we talked about coming to our Promised Land.

At the end of the meeting, the diggers vowed that if any man is arrested for not having his licence, they will all rise up and rescue him from the lockup. Then little fires spurted across Bakery Hill as the diggers burned their licences. It looked really pretty, like the red and gold lanterns that I once saw inside the Chinese shop. (That seems so long ago now.)

Thursday 30 November 1854

My father said a strange thing this morning, Jennychen, as we were walking together towards the creek. Actually, us walking together was strange in itself, for usually Vati sets off at dawn with Sancho Panza and Alphonse and J J, and then I go a bit later to get Tulip for them. But today my father waited for me, and he took my hand as we made our way through the diggings. I thought he must want to talk to me about something, but he was very quiet. And then as we were to part—as he was to go to the mine, and I was to go to the horse paddock—he said, 'Keep your eyes and ears open, Rosa. I have a feeling that you are to witness History in the making.' That was all he said. And when I took Tulip back, he was already down the shaft.

But I have vowed to try to write everything down for you, Jennychen, in case something does happen and I fail to see its importance. I must say, there is not much History going on at the moment, for there is just a boring old licence hunt starting, and we have them every second day. (Have I told you that the redcoats always ride out now, as well as the police?)

We are to have a full rehearsal this afternoon, on the Performance Space. (We won't have the horses of course, for they will be working. But we have become so accustomed to pretending we are riding them that sometimes I imagine I can hear their hooves upon the earth.) The good news is that it is going to be all right about the costumes, for darling Miss du Val has promised to lend us some cloaks! I personally think it will look even better, if we are all in different colours as we ride out, than if we were all in matching blue. Only four days to go till Sunday!

I can hear some bullets going off in the licence hunt. Today the cavalry are massed around the police, as if they are ready for a battle. Yet as the diggers are not lined up against them, they look pretty silly. Commissioner Rede is there, in his coat with gold braid, and he is waving a piece of paper. He sounds as if he is trying to shout something out, but his horse keeps rearing. Wouldn't you think the Government would get a Commissioner who knew how to ride properly?

Midday

The diggers are all very angry because eight men were arrested in this morning's licence hunt. They are all rushing up to Bakery Hill. I can see our flag going up the pole . . .

Will go and see what is happening.

Later

It turns out that poor Sancho Panza was one of the men arrested, and the Government will not allow the prisoners free on bail! I feel so sorry for him, stuck in the lockup. I wonder if they are making him wear leg irons like the convicts.

At the meeting, the diggers vowed to defend themselves from any further licence hunts. Mr Lalor got up on the stump and asked the diggers to choose their own Captains, and form ranks.

My father gave Mama a kiss, and then he bent down so that he was the same height as me. 'Look after your mother for me, Rosa,' he said. And before I could realise what was happening, he had joined the Company that has Raffy as its leader.

Now about a thousand men are marching down the Main Road towards the Eureka field. Captain Ross is at their head, and he is carrying the banner of the Southern Cross. Beside him is Mr Lalor.

Mama seems very upset, as if Vati has left us and gone a million miles away, but I have just seen him march past. Katie's father joined the Company that has Danny's father as its Captain. I said I would meet her at the creek paddock, so will finish this later.

Night time

I am so upset, Jennychen, that I barely feel like writing. When Katie and I left the creek and went to the Performance Space this afternoon, we found that our lovely open area had been taken over by the Companies of diggers! They had built a sort of fence around it, made out of wooden slabs, and some of the Companies were drilling like soldiers (except most of the men carried sticks instead of muskets). I saw my father marching about, and called out to him, but he just waved and kept on going *left-right-left-right-about-turn*.

At dusk all the men marched back up the Main Road to Bakery Hill, and once again they hoisted the banner to the top of the flagpole. Mama would not allow me to go to the meeting, but Danny Hayes says that the men all gathered around the flagpole and swore an oath on the Southern Cross, to stand by each other and fight to defend their liberty. Then they took the flag down again, and marched back to their Stockade on the Eureka field.

Our camp is very lonely, for Alphonse and J J have also gone down to the Eureka field, and there is only Mama and me here. It has started to rain, and Mama is fretting about Vati not having his oilskin coat or any blankets, but I think it serves him right. Maybe if he gets really cold and wet he will come home again.

Friday 1 December 1854

Morning

Vati did come home last night, but it was after I had gone to bed. I heard him and Mama quietly talking. He was gone again by the time I got up this morning. Weather has cleared, and I can see the Southern Cross flying above the Stockade.

Left-right-left-right-left-right-about-turn . . .

Sometimes on the breeze I can hear the men drilling. Of course, you would not normally be able to hear voices from the Eureka field, but today none of the diggers have gone to work. It is silent as a Sunday, without the noise of the cradles and the windlasses.

Haec scribens interpellata sum . . . Katie and Maeve and Colleen have arrived, so I will stop!

Later

We went to Town to visit Miss du Val to ask her what to do about our Performance. We thought she might be able to suggest another place where we could do it. But we did not manage to see her because there were so many police around. First they were making the diggers all get out of the Hotels, and then they were making them get off the streets and go back to their tents. We saw them arrest two men and take them away to the lockup.

Then one of the Joes grabbed Katie by the arm.

'Where do you think you are going?' he shouted at us.

'Nowhere,' Katie told him.

'Well go nowhere somewhere else!' And the policeman shooed us back down the main road as if we were a flock of chickens.

By then it was dinnertime, so I took some damper and cold chops down to the Stockade for Vati.

Left-right-left-right-left-right-about-turn . . .

The Companies were all drilling around and around, and the space inside the Stockade is only about as big as a cricket field, so the men kept on nearly bumping into each other. Most of them still do not have any rifles, but there is a blacksmith there making pikes.

Vati came over to the fence to get the food. (The slabs of wood reach only as high as my shoulder.) 'How are you, *liebchen*?' he asked.

I wanted to talk to my father about how our Performance Space has been taken over and how it is not fair after we gave the diggers our material for the flag, but I knew he would think I was being silly, so I just said I was good and I went to Katie's tent. (It is within spitting distance of the southern fence of the Stockade.)

We spent the afternoon trying to think of other places to have the Performance. Because of the horses, it is very difficult. (I think I explained, Jennychen, that

there are mine shafts and old holes and mounds of
earth over most of the diggings, so a horse would be in
danger of breaking its leg.) Danny and the boys seem to
have lost interest anyway in the Performance. They
spend all their time practising drilling, in the hope that
the men will allow them to join the Stockade. Or else
they roam down the Melbourne Road, so that when
more soldiers come they can throw stones and shout
again. I am sick of boys and men and soldiers.

Night
My father came back after dark. He says that different
Companies are taking it in turns to do sentry duty, and
it will be his turn tomorrow night. He was too tired to
eat his supper, and has gone to bed already.

Saturday 2 December 1854
Once again this morning my father was gone before I
awoke. Again, there is a strange Sunday feeling here in
Ballarat, as the mines are idle and the diggers are sitting
about their camps. Of course, down at the Stockade
there are only a few hundred gathered, but the others
will not work until whatever is going to happen,
happens. But nobody seems to know what that is, or
when it will be.

Katie and I went to Father Pat's for our Latin

lesson, around 10 o'clock. We did not know if we were meant to, but he greeted us kindly and heard our verbs. He looks sad and tired. At the end of the lesson he went into the Chapel, and Katie and I asked Joannes what was wrong. He told us that Father Pat has gone twice to Commissioner Rede to plead that the licence hunts stop for a short time, to allow everybody to calm down. But Father Pat told Joannes that the Commissioner will not give an inch, and seems to be wanting trouble.

When Father Pat came out of the Chapel, Katie and I went with him to the Stockade, where he talked to the diggers. He warned them against being violent, and he pointed to Katie and me and asked the men if they wanted to see the blood of innocent children shed. Then he talked about turning the other cheek if the Government comes.

At that point my father walked over to the fence where I was standing, so I didn't hear any more.

'What is happening?' I asked.

'Nothing much,' my father told me.

'What's going to happen?'

'I don't know,' Vati said. 'Nothing until Monday, I imagine.' He explained that the soldiers never come out on licence hunts on Saturdays or Sundays.

I suddenly had an idea. If nothing is going to happen tomorrow, why couldn't we still do the

Performance, where we had planned? Then all the men in the Stockade could watch, and it would be more interesting for them than drilling!

I did not mention the idea to my father, in case he said 'No'. But I went and told Katie, and she thought it was a great idea. We decided to wait until dinnertime tomorrow, and then spring it upon Raffy as a surprise. He is sure to agree, and as he is one of the Captains, then Mr Lalor will have to let us do it. And by tomorrow afternoon all the diggers will be so sick of marching around in circles with sticks that they will love to see our circus and play.

We felt so excited that we went and found Danny and the other boys, and we all spent the afternoon at the creek paddock, rehearsing the whole program. It was wonderful today, because we had the horses, and also the coloured cloaks which we have borrowed from Miss du Val. Everything went perfectly, and even Colleen remembered her lines.

Now it is nearly dark. Most of the diggers have left the Stockade and gone home to their families, but of course Vati has to be on sentry duty until tomorrow morning. Mama does not mind because Mrs Flanagan and the girls are coming here to stay for the night. (Mr Flanagan is on sentry duty too.)

They will be here any minute!

(Written Monday 4 December)

Oh Jennychen, when I wrote to you so long ago about coming to live in Upside Down Land, I swear I had no idea what it would feel like if the world actually turned upside down. But now I know. I know too what my father meant about seeing History being made. But I have learned that when History really is happening all around you, there is no time for writing it down. At the moment there seems to be a little space of quiet, so I will try to begin to tell you what has been happening. I will go back to the time when Katie and her mother and sisters arrived on Saturday night, and I will attempt to forget what has happened since, and set things down, just as they occurred . . .

Saturday night continued . . .

Katie, Maeve, Colleen, and her mother arrive, just after Mama and I have finished supper. (Well, I have finished mine, but Mama has barely touched her chop.) I put the kettle on the fire and we all have a cup of tea, and then we girls play charades until Mama says it is time for us to go to sleep. So Katie snuggles into my cot with me, and Maeve and Colleen have a little nest on the floor. And I fall asleep.

I am woken by a scream.

Perhaps at first I think it is some sort of night bird, it is so piercing and strange. And then my mind jumps to the Stockade, and I think that something terrible has happened there, despite what everyone says about how nothing can happen until Monday.

But the terrible sound is far closer than the Eureka field, it is right inside the tent, and as I wake fully I realise that it is my mother who is screaming.

Katie is sitting bolt upright beside me in the bed. 'The baby has started!' she announces.

I know that you, Jennychen, are as accustomed to babies as is Katie Flanagan, so will not tell you how terrible they are (while they are being born, I mean). I will just say that my mother screams and screams, while Mrs Flanagan boils up two kettles of water on the fire and rips a good bedsheet into bandages.

How long does it go on before Mrs Flanagan suddenly tells Katie and me to run for Doctor Carr? I do not know.

But we take the lamp and run up the Main Road towards Town. As we reach the bridge over the Yarrowee, two soldiers loom out from the shadows and grab us so roughly that I think the flame in the lamp will go out. I am so breathless I cannot speak at first, but Katie explains our mission.

It is of no avail. Although I tell the redcoats that my mother needs the doctor, they will not allow us to pass across the bridge and enter the Town. We have no choice but to return.

When we arrive back at the tent, we find Danny Hayes's mother there, and also Mrs Tredinnick. That feels safer, somehow. But although I know that the women are more useful than my father could be, I wish that he were here too, and not on sentry duty.

My mother's screams go on and on, piercing the night. Mrs Flanagan sends us girls outside to keep the fire going, and the kettles boiling. We have our blankets with us, and after a while Katie and her sisters curl up against the stack of firewood, but I sit with the fire, pushing the big log in as it burns down. I can see the silhouettes of the women, thrown by the lamplight against the canvas of the tent.

And I know that I will not sleep no matter how long this night takes.

Sunday 3 December 1854
(Written Monday 4 December)

Saturday changes to Sunday as the hours go on.

How long is it really?

I do not know. But it seems like the most endless amount of time that I spend, watching the silhouettes, listening to the screams cut through the night, wondering if my mother will die—or when my mother will die—before I suddenly know what it is that I must do.

I push the big log into the coals again, check that the kettles are full and bubbling, then—clutching my grey blanket around me like a cloak—I set off through the darkness towards the Eureka field. This time I take no lamp, for there may be more soldiers posted around the diggings as spies, and this time I do not intend to be sent back.

The night is dark, Jennychen, for the moon is just a tiny fingernail in the sky. Yet that is good, I tell myself, for that means that the Southern Cross blazes all the more brightly above me. As I pick my way through the tents and camp sites, towards the road, I think back to that night on the ship, when we crossed the Line, and I first saw my wishing stars, and I remember my father's arms holding me and Mama safe as Mama talked of the Promised Land, and I know (or I tell myself that I know) that soon the three of us will be safe together again.

Any minute now . . .

I look back across the Gravel Pits, and can just make out the faint light of our tent. All the other tents are in darkness, there and on the Eureka field.

By the time that I reach the turning into the Melbourne Road, my eyes have become accustomed to the blackness. Or perhaps the very first rays of dawn are starting.

I trot on, feeling the road beneath my bare feet, passing the darkened ruin of what was once the Eureka Hotel. Not long now . . .

By the first grey light of dawn I am able to see the fence. It looks so frail and makeshift that it has the appearance of an old ruin from a derelict farm. Or perhaps it is because everything is so quiet that the Stockade appears deserted.

I creep around the fence, towards where I think my father will be doing sentry duty. I want him to know that it is me coming, and not a soldier from the Government, and so I try to think of a song to sing. But my mind is empty of tunes. Then I seem to hear my voice as if it is the voice of somebody else, and it is reciting very softly:

> *It is an Ancient Mariner,*
> *And he stoppeth one of three.*
> *'By thy long beard and glittering eye,*
> *Now wherefore stopp'st thou me?'*

As I walk on, and the story of the poem unfolds, I am aware how silent the dawn is, for no birds are awake yet, and how still the air is, for the flag hangs limp from the pole.

Alone, alone, all, all, alone,
Alone on a wide wide sea!
And never a saint took pity on
My soul in agony.

How can I write down the next bit? I do not know, Jennychen. I do not know how it happened.

At the time, all I know is that I am walking, touching the fence with one hand, and reciting softly.

'Rosa?'

Do I hear my father's voice quietly say my name?

Do I see my father first?

Or do I first see the shadows that suddenly loom out of the blackness, as the two shadows of the soldiers on the bridge of the Yarrowee loomed earlier tonight?

Yet this time it is not *two* soldiers but *twenty, thirty, forty*—I do not know how many—soldiers that loom against the dark grey light of the dawn.

I hear a gun.

No, I see a gun, as my father fires it into the air, to sound the alarm.

Another gun goes off, almost simultaneously.

And then the screaming and the noise makes the earlier screams of my mother seem as nothing, and the dawn seems to break in a moment as the redcoats and the bluecoats swarm upon the Stockade, and my father lifts me up and over the fence, and the next thing I know I am alone and lying in a kind of dark little cave, underneath a pile of slabs, and I am looking out and seeing—

Oh, Jennychen, I cannot tell you much of what I am seeing, for everything is going on at the same time, and words do not seem to work for the noise of the bullets and the smell of burning and the sight of blood gushing as men run at each other with bayonets.

Where is my father?

That is my main thought.

I cannot see him anywhere.

But I do see Mr Lalor climb onto a little earth mound, and I hear him yelling to the diggers, and I see him spin around as a bullet hits him in the arm. As he falls to the ground, I see two diggers grab hold of his body, and they carry it swiftly to where I am hiding, and they push him into my little cave beneath the slabs. I am sure they do not even see me. I try to make a sort of bandage from my petticoat, and tie it around and around Mr Lalor's arm, to stop the blood spouting, and I tuck my blanket around him, for he is shivering. But he does not seem to know that I am with him.

Where is my father?

That is all I can think as the redcoats and the bluecoats swarm in on foot, and more redcoats on horses are riding around the fence in a semicircle.

Where is my father?

That is all I can think as I see the lemonade man struck by a bullet in the mouth.

Where is my father?

That is all I can think as I watch Captain Ross who stands for one last moment, so proud in his red sash, at the foot of the flagpole, before he shudders to the ground.

I watch too as a bluecoat hauls down the Southern Cross, cuts the flag from its rope, and drapes it around his own shoulders as some sort of trophy.

Where is my father? I think.

If the hours of my mother's screaming that night seemed to go on for an eternity, the time of the battle seems to pass in one crowded moment (though I have since been told that it lasted for fifteen minutes).

Then there is a time (which people say went on for an hour) of burning and rampage, as the soldiers and the police storm right through the Eureka field, attacking families in their camps, setting fire to tents, stealing gold from out of the diggers' pockets. (From my little cave I can smell the burning, hear the screaming.)

At the same time, within the fence of the Stockade, I see police and soldiers rounding up any men who can walk, and taking them as prisoners.

That is when at last I see my father.

He is limping badly, and covered in mud, and I am about to run out from my bolthole to him but he looks over towards the pile of slabs, and makes a motion with his head which I know means: *No. Stay there.*

And so I do.

As I watch that first lot of prisoners being led away, I also see the familiar figure of Father Pat, moving among those diggers who lie wounded on the ground. He is bending over, speaking to each one, but now a Joe bails him up with a bayonet and starts shouting at the Priest that he is to leave the Stockade immediately. He has no choice but to obey.

To my great joy, I see the Priest taking a path that will lead him past my hideaway. By now the Joe who threatened him has gone to join the others with the prisoners, and I call out *Psssst*, and I manage to attract the attention of Father Pat ...

Monday 4 December 1854

I must stop this episode of my story at this point, dear Jennychen. There are many chores that must be done here. Mrs Flanagan is very kind, but has her own troubles, for Katie's father is in the lockup with Vati and the other prisoners. (There are one hundred and fouteen men imprisoned, and people are saying that many of them were not even in the Stockade at the time of the battle. As well, Mr Seekamp was arrested this morning, for writing Sedition in the newspaper.)

Mrs Tredinninck is our main helper—for as she says, she had no man to lose in the battle. The baby is still poorly, as is Mama. She has called him Ross, after Captain Ross, for she was very saddened to hear of the brave Canadian's death.

Later

Katie and I were at Mrs McTavish's store this afternoon when we heard the muffled beating of a funeral drum.

Most of the dead from the Stockade were hastily buried yesterday (did I tell you that people say that the count of diggers killed is as high as twenty-two?) but some bodies were taken away, and had a proper burial today.

'It is the funeral of that poor wee Canadian laddie,' Mrs McTavish murmured.

Clutching our brown paper packages of tea and flour, and a string bag full of potatoes and onions, Katie and I ran out to the Main Road, where we saw Danny Hayes beating out the slow dismal rhythm on the black-shrouded drum. Behind him stretched a procession of about five hundred diggers, marching three abreast.

Despite our groceries we tagged onto the rear, and marched on in silence, up the road, and over the bridge that spans the Yarrowee. I felt my heart jump as we took the turn towards the Government Camp, and marched around the fortifications. The sentries of course pretended not to see us, but no-one inside that place could have failed to hear the slow message of the drum.

Naturally, I could not but think of my father inside the Camp, in the gaol. Oh, I am so afraid for his safety, Jennychen. I have been trying to concentrate upon writing this journal, and doing my chores, to keep from thinking about what his fate may be. But all sorts of terrible rumours are flying about. Some people are saying that the soldiers are digging a huge pit, where they intend to bury the prisoners alive. Others maintain that a gallows has been erected, and the diggers will all be hanged without Trial. Truly, I cannot bear to think on it . . .

After we circled the Camp, we turned into the Creswick Road, and marched on to the cemetery, where Mr Humffray spoke a beautiful oration, calling Captain Ross 'the Bridegroom of the Flag'. I so wished that we had the banner to put over his coffin, but of course the police took it away in triumph, after the battle. And then I remembered Mrs Tredinnick . . .

Dumping my bag of vegetables onto Katie, I ran to

the bush that surrounds the graveyard, and plucked an armful of late-flowering wattle. As I arrived back at the graveside, Mr Humffray and some other men were already throwing earth upon the coffin. So I scattered the golden flowers into the Captain's grave.

It is evening now, and I must go and run an Errand for Father Pat. I dare not write down my purpose, for there are still spies about, and the police have ransacked some of the tents, looking for Certain Diggers who made good their escape yesterday. I fear to say more, lest they go through our tent and take this journal.

Tuesday 5 December 1854

Midday

Katie and I had a Latin lesson this morning. Then we had to go up to Town, to run a Message for Father Pat.

On the way back, we made our way to the fortification fence that surrounds the Government Camp. We were hoping that we might be able to see our fathers, perhaps exercising on the parade ground. But our hopes were in vain, for all the prisoners are locked away inside a big storehouse. We did however see Miss du Val in the street, and she told us not to believe the rumours of the pit and the gallows. She says that the first men are already being taken before the Magistrates. Katie and I felt a bit more cheerful when she said that, for it means that the prisoners are at least not going to be executed without Trial. We told her we are really sorry about Mr Seekamp.

Mama was also pleased to hear that the prisoners are starting to go before the Court. Though now there are rumours that some men are to be charged with High Treason, and we fear lest Vati is among them. (As you know, that carries the Death Penalty.)

One good thing is that poor Mama is so worried about Ross that she has not much time to fret about my father. He is very thin and coughs through the night (my brother, I mean), and he does not seem to keep the milk down. Mrs Hayes has brought some of her special remedies.

Haec scribens interpellata sum . . . Katie has arrived to say that Father Pat wants to give us some extra Latin homework . . .

Evening

This afternoon Katie and I spied a huge cloud of dust coming up the road from Melbourne. We barely had time to wonder what it could be before we heard the sounds of a military band, and then we watched with heavy hearts as a whole new contingent of soldiers marched through the diggings, and into Ballarat. Danny said he counted eight hundred men on foot, as well as the cavalry brigades. There were also four cannon, and dozens of waggons carrying enough ammunition to win a battle in the Crimea. Mrs Tredinnick was speaking to another lady at the butcher's, and she said that Major General Sir Robert Nickle himself has arrived. That is the Commander of all the forces in the Colony, whom Governor Hotham has sent to be in charge here. Mama is fearful lest this means that the soldiers will ride out from the Camp again, and attack us all.

I can hear poor Ross as I write this. Mrs Hayes's remedies do not seem to be working. Mama fears lest he has whooping cough.

Thursday 7 December 1854

My father is home again! He went before the Court this afternoon, but all the evidence was so muddled up that the Magistrate had to let him go. Vati says that the cases are a complete shambles, with police spies telling so many lies that they do not know what they are saying. I think his wound is still troubling him, for he is limping very badly, and when he does not think I am looking, I can see him wincing for the pain. But at the same time, I have never seen him so happy. He even made me sit on his lap and he rocked me back and forth, like he used to do when I was a little girl.

Am too happy to write any more.

Friday 8 December 1854

Poor Ross coughed again through the night. Mama and Vati took turns nursing him. They tried all the remedies, but nothing seems to work.

I have decided to go and do something about the situation.

Later

Dr Wong has just left. He says that Ross has colic, but is otherwise healthy, and it is Mama who needs strengthening. He brought some of those mysterious things from his glass jars, and he showed me how to boil them up to make a medicine for my mother to drink.

He also examined my father's leg wound. Then he shook his head, and looked really serious. I thought he was going to say that the leg would have be amputated. But he announced that he fears Vati will not be able to return to goldmining for a long time.

'Thank heavens for small mercies!' said Mama. She could not stop smiling after the doctor's visit.

Saturday 9 December 1854

After this morning's Latin lesson, Katie and I went to the *Latibulum*. It was too hot to pan for gold, so we started to make our swimming hole bigger, by taking rocks out of the bottom and building a dam wall.

Forgot to tell you! Mr Flanagan was let out of prison yesterday, but Katie says that he does not want to return to digging. Well, not for gold. She says that he is talking of becoming a farmer. (Some people are saying that the Governor may now feel that he has to open up the land for farming. These past few days there have been meetings all over Victoria, demanding land, and the end of licence fees, and a Republic, and the right to vote. Vati said it is all a result of the diggers standing up for themselves at the Stockade, and the deaths were not in vain.)

Before we came home we dug up our matchbox of *aurum*. We plan to take it to one of the merchants in Town on Monday.

Monday 11 December 1854

Katie and I are to sell our *aurum* this morning. I have decided to use my share of the money to buy a present for Ross. He slept right through the night, without coughing at all. Ever since Mama has started drinking Dr Wong's medicine, my baby brother has been getting better too. I swear he smiled at me earlier. He has really strong fingers, and the sweetest little toes.

Evening

The Magistrate trials are over. Thirteen men have been charged with High Treason (as well as the Sedition charge against Mr Seekamp). Danny's father is among the thirteen, as is Raffy. Also the black man, Mr Joseph, who sometimes came to our reading group. My father is of course very worried for them all. He says that Governor Hotham will be determined to make an Example of them, and that if any of the thirteen are convicted, they will surely be hanged.

'Can nothing be done to save them?' I asked.

'We must put our faith in the people,' Vati said.

He means the Juries, in whose hands the fate of the prisoners will rest.

Tuesday 12 December 1854

We watched this morning as a big contingent of soldiers escorted the fourteen prisoners down the road to Melbourne, where they shall be tried before a Judge and Jury. Poor Mrs Hayes ran out from the crowd at the roadside. She had her youngest baby in her arms, and the other little ones at her skirts, but the soldiers would not let them near Mr Hayes to kiss him farewell. Even Danny was crying. Miss du Val was also there, watching as her husband went past. Her face was strong as a statue.

I thought how I would have felt if my father had not been released, and I know how truly lucky we are. I still wear my little charm, and I wonder if this was perhaps the sort of riches that the Chinese gentleman was talking about. I mean, to be standing in the sunshine with my father and my mother and my new baby brother. (Oh! I forgot to say. The dust in the matchbox proved to be what they call Fool's Gold.)

Sunday 31 December 1854
Mrs Wood's Private Board and Lodging House
Little Collins Street East, Melbourne

Vati has bought me a most beautiful journal for the New Year, with creamy paper and a green leather binding and a brass lock with a little key, so I have decided to fill the last few pages of this poor old friend, and then post it off to you, Jennychen. In truth, I have neglected my journal-writing these last couple of weeks, for we have been so busy with the move to Melbourne.

Yes, we are back at Mrs Wood's, but this time we are all together in our own room. Mama is keen for us to find somewhere more spacious, but Vati says that this place is convenient. (He has already obtained a position with the *Argus*. With his gammy leg, he does not want to walk far to work.)

The trials of the Ballarat prisoners have not begun, and indeed my father says that they may not take place for some months. When they do, he will be writing about them for the paper (and will no doubt send his reports to your father, as well).

Mama and I went back to Bourke Street the other day, where all the drapers' and tailors' shops are. She put notices in some of the windows, advertising her services for dressmaking and fine mending. And this time we went *into* the Synagogue, and had a look. It is as if my mother too has changed, as a result of the last few months. She is more like my father. I mean, she does more of what she wants to do. But it is also as if she is more like herself. (Or perhaps it is just that I know her a little bit better.)

Now that we are away from the diggings, and the fear of spies, I can at last let you into my Secret. (I wonder—have you guessed, Jennychen?)

But if I am to tell you, first you must turn back to where I left my tale on the morning of Sunday December 3. (That seems a lifetime ago, although it is only four weeks!)

Sunday 3 December 1854 continued . . .
As you will remember, I am lying in my little hole, underneath a pile of slabs, with the digger's leader Mr

Peter Lalor lying unconscious beside me. I have bandaged up his bleeding arm with my petticoat, and have tucked my blanket around him.

By now the actual battle is over, and the police have rounded up the prisoners (including Vati), but the butchery and the burning goes on. Peeping out through a crack between the slabs, I see Father Pat moving among the wounded. I see the Joe order him to leave, and I call the Priest over . . .

'*Pssssst!*'

At first I fear that he will walk by without hearing, so at the risk of giving away the hiding place, I call again. '*Pssssst!*' Then I add one of our Latin exclamations. '*Heus!*' (It sounds like a sneeze.)

The Priest appears to be bending down to get a pebble from his boot, but the next thing I know he is calling softly. 'Rosa! Is that you?'

I whisper that it is, and that Mr Lalor is with me, and is badly wounded.

Father Pat promises that he will work out some way of rescue. 'Be patient, my child,' he tells me. As he turns to go, he raises a finger and holds it to his lips, as if to seal our secrecy. '*Secretum!*' he whispers.

'*Secretum,*' I whisper back. I remember what the Priest once said, about how he was good at keeping secrets, and I feel that Mr Lalor and I are in safe hands.

It seems an age that I wait. The screaming inside and outside the Stockade begins to subside, as through the crack I see the bodies of the dead being carted away. Finally the last of the soldiers and police leave. Smoke still drifts through the air, for in many places the grass around the tents has caught on fire.

At last I hear a muffled sound of footsteps—or is it hoofs?—and then I hear the most welcome sound of—yes! It is dear Tulip, and behind Tulip there is our sledge, piled with sticks and dead leaves. *How strange*, I think. Who would be collecting kindling for the fire at this time—and inside the battlefield?

And then as Tulip moves her head, I see Katie, holding the halter.

(Later, I discover that Father Pat was afraid that he would attract too much attention if he himself were to come back to the Stockade. But who ever notices a couple of children? And the sight of Katie and me collecting firewood was a fairly common one.)

Luckily, by now Mr Lalor seems to be waking from his coma, and so I am able to explain to him what we plan to do. Katie and I wait until we are sure that no-one is looking. Then we quickly move the slabs, and bustle the diggers' leader onto the sledge. We tuck the old grey blanket around him, and quickly cover him up with branches and leaves. Taking hold of Tulip's halter, we begin to move towards a gap, where the timber fence of the Stockade has been knocked down . . .

'*What the hell do you two think you're doing?*'

We are nearly past the last of the tents of the Eureka field when we hear the voice shouting from behind. Swinging around, we see one of the Joes running fast towards us (or as fast as he can run, with his big belly wobbling in front of him).

'*What have you girls got in that sledge?*' He is so close that I can smell the rum on his breath. I feel myself trembling. I can see the dried blood on the policeman's bayonet as he starts to poke it towards the pile of branches that are thinly covering the diggers' leader.

Suddenly there is another voice. A voice so dripping in sweetness that it would mellow even the heart of a Ballarat Joe. 'Cannot you see, sir, that my friends and I are simply gathering firewood to take home to our poor mothers?' Salvation tosses her thick blonde plait from one shoulder to the other, and gazes innocently from her wide blue eyes. Dressed up in her Sunday clothes, she is as neat and clean as I am untidy and filthy.

'Come on, girls, we have our chores to do.' I watch in astonishment as Salvation beams again at our enemy, then takes the halter rope from me, and proceeds to lead Tulip with her precious cargo away from danger, and towards the line of wattle that fringes the bush. The policeman does not seem to know what to do. Neither for a moment do Katie or I. Then, gathering our wits, we scamper off in Salvation's wake.

'Thank you,' Katie and I both say when at last we are safe. And then for a moment we all stand looking at each other. After all the ill feeling that there has been, I do not know what else to say to Salvation.

'You had better hurry on your way,' Sal tells us, 'or the police might come looking for whoever you have hidden there.' And with that she tosses her plait, and runs back towards the diggings.

Katie shrugs at me, and I suddenly see that those two are really quite alike. I could imagine them being great friends, if they were not enemies.

One thing is sure: we had better make good our escape. And so I grab the halter rope again.

Where do we take the fugitive?

Where else but the *Latibulum*—our special Hiding Place?

I am rapidly running out of space in this journal, so for the rest of this tale I will simply tell you that later in that dreadful day (at about the time that our Grande Performance would have been) we brought Father Pat to the Hidden Valley. I am not quite sure what happened after that, but by the Monday night, Mr Lalor was at the Priest's house in Ballarat. By this time the shot-wound in his arm had become gangrenous, and Katie and I were sent to fetch Doctor Doyle, who amputated the limb. After this, Mr Lalor was forced to stay and rest for a few days, before moving on to another safe house. The Governor was so determined to catch the diggers' leader that he posted a Reward of two hundred pounds for anyone who would give information leading to his arrest. But neither then nor since has anyone come forward to peach on Mr Lalor.

As you have probably guessed, Jennychen, during the time that the fugitive stayed with the Priest, Katie and I ran messages for him. Nobody suspected us, you see, because we carried our Grammar Books, and if anyone asked what we were doing, we just said that we were on our way to a lesson with Father Pat. And what could sound more innocent than Latin?

Epilogue

The Belle Vue Boarding House
Lydiard Street
Ballarat

Monday 3 December 1855

Meine liebe Jennychen,

We have come up from Melbourne for a few days, as this afternoon there was the Memorial Meeting, to mark the first anniversary of the event which everybody now calls 'the Eureka Stockade'.

It seems strange to be spending the night in Ballarat Town, and not to be on the Gravel Pits, under canvas. Katie invited me to stay with her, but Mama said that Ross's first birthday is a Family Occasion, and we should all be together.

Yes, the Flanagans are still living in the Hidden Valley, although it is hardly hidden any more. The track is well worn, for Katie's father brings milk into Town every day of the week, and often other produce as well. They have five cows now, as well as a couple of pigs and a dozen hens—and dear Tulip, whom I saw too of course, when I went to visit Katie. I think she is liking her new life as a farmhorse. (Mrs Flanagan told

Mama it was the best luck in the world that the 'gold' that Katie and I found proved to be worthless, and Mr Flanagan decided to take up a farming lease on the rich pastures beside the little creek.)

Katie and Sal have worked hard on the swimming hole, and it is now so deep that you can sit in water right up to your neck, or float comfortably on your back. I took Ross for his first paddle there. He is fat as butter, and Mama says he is such an easygoing child that she is taking more and more orders for dressmaking. I look forward to the time when he is older and I can use him in plays.

Did I tell you that some of my schoolfriends and I did the Judith play as a concert for our class? It went very well, and I am thinking that while we are in Ballarat it might be possible to put on our Grande Performance at last. After all, Raffy is here, and also Danny Hayes and most of the other boys, and Salvation could have a part as well. (She has changed her opinion about plays, Katie reports. And probably about many things, now that she is Katie's friend.) If we were to do it, I am sure that Miss du Val would again be willing to lend us the cloaks.

Katie is still doing Elocution classes with her. That is no doubt why she was chosen to open the Memorial Meeting with the recitation of one of the many poems that have been written about the battle . . .

A banner bold of white and blue
Above the flimsy Stockade flew
As from the darkness soldiers came.
The British Governor bears the blame
For all the blood that spilled that night
Beneath the starry banner bright . . .

Everybody said that they could hear, although the crowd
was so vast that it quite filled our old Performance Space. After
Katie was finished, Father Pat gave a blessing. Then Mr Lalor
made a speech. (Did I tell you that he is now in Parliament,
representing Ballarat? So is Mr Humffray. There isn't a
Republic yet, but the diggers did win the vote.) Danny Hayes's
father spoke next, and then Raffy. Everybody cheered when he
was introduced as 'our local Magistrate'—for he is a member of
the people's Court that has taken the place of the old gold-lace
Commissioners. And people cheered again when Raffy
reminded everyone that just a couple of weeks ago Sir Charles
Hotham was forced to resign as Governor. (You know,
Jennychen, I sometimes think about that albatross that he shot,
and wonder if that was the beginning of all this Misfortune.)

My father's mates Alphonse and Sancho Panza and J J
were in the crowd with us (they are mining in Bendigo now, and
are certain that they are going to make their fortunes before the
year is out). So all in all it was quite like Old Times—except of
course for those who were not there (like poor Captain Ross, and

Mr Thonen who used to make such delicious lemonade).

When all the yabber yabber was over, Raffy began selling copies of a book that he has written about what happened here a year ago. Of course we bought a copy. (Raffy wrote in it: For Rosa—Who Helped to Make the Flag. I felt so proud.)

As you know, my father has not yet had time to finish his own book, and on the way back from the meeting, I dared to ask him if he minds that the story of the Stockade has already been published.

'Not at all, liebchen,' my father smiled. 'For the tale of Eureka will be told and retold, time and again, through our lifetimes, and down through the ages.'

Vati took my hand as we walked up the slope of Bakery Hill, where the Southern Cross was first flown, and I found myself remembering something he had said one morning, as we were walking together to the mine. 'So did we see History at Eureka?' I asked.

'History?' my father laughed. 'Well—maybe a Legend.'

As we reached the crest of the hill, I looked up and saw the banner again, white against blue. But this time it seemed to stretch as far as the eye could see.

HISTORICAL NOTE

Nobody is quite sure how the gold got into the land. There were no people around to write history, in those long ago days when the earth was bubbling away, finding its shape. Yet somehow, in the corner of a southern continent, some of the quartz that rippled across the crust of the planet contained dust and little stones that were a dirty yellow colour. After these rivers cooled and settled, layers of soil began to cover them. Sometimes close to the surface, sometimes deep below, the ancient golden creek beds lay hidden.

Then the Kulin came to care for the land. One of the many places where they liked to stay was a fertile valley, well stocked with meat and plant food, and watered by a creek they named 'Yarrowee'. They showed their appreciation of this camping ground in the name 'Ballarat', which meant 'Good Resting Place'. For thousands of years, the Kulin regularly stayed there. They improved the pastures by burning. They obeyed the laws of the land. Sometimes they saw soft yellow coloured stone, when they were digging for food, or even when they were getting water from the creek. However, their society was not based on yellow stones, and so they left this stuff in the ground where it belonged.

About two hundred years ago, very different people came to this corner of the continent. Their way of living was based on yellow stones, or on the paper money which was just another way of measuring these stones. At first, the white men did not know about the ancient creek beds that lay underneath the earth. They pushed the Kulin off the grasslands around Ballarat, so that they could make money out of cattle and sheep. But about a hundred and fifty years ago, people were starting to find golden dust, or even little lumps of gold.

At this time, Australia was not an independent country. It did not have its own flag, or its own national government. There were not any states. Instead, there were a number of colonies, ruled by the monarch of England. To each colony, the Queen (or her advisers in England) sent a man called a Governor, to govern or rule the people on her behalf. To help him make decisions, there was a small group of men called the Legislative Council, elected by a few rich squatters and merchants. But most men were not allowed to vote for who would run the government. And no women at all were allowed to vote. All of this meant that the Governor could make up any law he liked, and he could send the police and soldiers to enforce it.

In 1851, the south-eastern corner of the continent of Australia became a new colony, named 'Victoria', after the Queen of England. That same year, gold was found at various sites in the colony, including the valley on the banks of the Yarrowee. The Gold Rush began—as people from all over the world hurried to Victoria and began to dig the soil, in the hope of getting very rich very quickly. In September 1851, a couple of brothers dug for two days at Ballarat, and found 60 pounds of gold. Within days, there were 6,000 people camping on the Kulin's grassland, and burrowing away into the earth.

By the law of England, all the gold in the colony belonged to the Queen. So the Governor made people pay a monthly licence fee of thirty shillings, for the right to dig. From the start, the diggers resented paying the fee. They even more resented the way the police and soldiers treated them if they had no licence.

People in all the goldfields of Victoria were already fed up when the new Governor, Sir Charles Hotham, arrived to run the colony in June 1854. Although His Excellency assured his masters in England that he was ready and willing to suppress any riot, he began by telling the colonials that he believed that all power came from the people. For a couple of months, the diggers thought that their way of life was going to get better. But the Governor was almost looking for trouble, in order to show who was in charge. He was also determined to get as much money as possible out of the licence fees, in order to get rid of the colony's debt in a very short time.

In Ballarat and the other fields, the diggers became angry when the police started coming out on more and more licence hunts. But it was not just the thirty shillings a month that people resented. Why should the diggers pay most of the money that supported the colony, when they had no right to vote for the Legislative Council, and no right to say how that money was spent?

A lot of the miners came from America, where the people had already broken away from the British Empire, and established a republic. Another large group of miners came from Catholic Ireland, and had a longstanding grievance against being ruled by the British monarch. Amongst the English diggers, there were men called Chartists, who wanted to establish a democratic system of government, based on the principle that every man should have a vote. Then there were immigrants from Germany, France and Italy, who had been part of the socialist and nationalist revolutionary uprisings of 1848.

All of these different ideals and causes of resentment were bubbling away at all the Victorian goldfields. But when a digger was murdered one night near the Eureka Hotel at Ballarat, the diggers in that area decided that enough was enough. Why should they pay their licence fees, when the police did not even protect them from being hit on the head in the dark?

Rosa has told most of the rest of the story in her journal. Nearly all the men at her father's reading group were really part of the history that happened at Eureka. These include Peter Lalor, Raffaello Carboni, John Humffray, George and Alfred Black, John Joseph, Edward Thonen, Henry Seekamp, and Timothy Hayes. Father Patrick Smyth was also a very important participant in these events, and Miss Clara du Val was the leading actress of the Gravel Pits Theatre. Jennychen was also a real person. Her father—known as 'the Mohr' (the Moor) to his family and friends—is well known for a pamphlet called *The Communist Manifesto*, as well as books about political economy. In 1855 he wrote an account of the 'riot at Ballarat and the general revolutionary movement in the colony of Victoria' for a German newspaper called the *Neu Oder-Zeitung*.

The fact that, even in Europe, people were interested in this news item shows that, from the very beginning, it was clear that *something* very important happened inside a little fence on the Eureka goldfield, during fifteen minutes on a Sunday dawn in December 1854. A hundred and fifty years later, people still argue about what that *something* actually was.

Was this the beginning of democracy in Australia? Was it perhaps an attempt at making a republic? Was it simply a protest about paying taxes? Or was it maybe just a bunch of men, playing at soldiers? Or indeed, should we criticise the diggers because they were mining the land that belonged to the Kulin?

Some of the answers lie in part of the story that happened after Rosa stopped writing her 1854 journal. Within days of the battle, there were huge meetings across the colony. People's demands included: the right to vote; the right to farm some of the land that the squatters had taken from the Kulin; the release of the prisoners; changes to the administration of the goldfields; the establishment of a republic.

When the thirteen men charged with High Treason came to court in Melbourne in March 1855, on each occasion the jury declared the defendant innocent, even though it was clear that most of the accused had taken part in the battle. Thousands of people gathered in the streets to cheer when the prisoners were freed.

As a result of this widespread show of strength, the Governor was forced, within a few months of that December dawn, to abolish the monthly licence fees and give the diggers the right to vote. He also opened up some of the land to small farmers. The old corrupt rule of the gold commissioners was abolished, and diggers were allowed to elect the members of the courts that set conditions on the goldfields. By the end of 1855, Sir Charles Hotham had been forced to back down so far that he resigned as Governor. And on the last day of that year, he caught a chill and died.

If the story of Eureka quickly travelled as far as Europe, it was of course even better known across the Australian continent. Over the next decades, whenever and wherever people stood up for their rights, they spoke of the Stockade, and the flag of the Southern Cross. When the Australian Federation of Labour was formed in 1889, the following lines of poetry were written for the occasion:

> *Fling out the Flag! And let friends and foes behold, for*
> *gain or loss,*
> *The sign of our faith and the fight we fight, the Stars of*
> *the Southern Cross!*
> *Oh! Blue's for the sky that is fair for all, whoever,*
> *wherever he be,*
> *And silver's the light that shines on all for hope and for*
> *liberty,*
> *And that's the desire that burns in our hearts, for ever*
> *quenchless and bright,*
> *And that's the sign of our flawless faith and the glorious*
> *fight we fight!* [1]

At that time in Australian history, there was a lot of poverty and unemployment, and working people across the land were struggling to defend their right to fair pay and fair conditions. It was out of these struggles that the trade union movement and the Australian Labor Party would be formed. In 1891, in a little place called Barcaldine in Queensland, striking shearers flew the Eureka flag and wore tiny Southern Cross banners. It was at this time that Henry Lawson wrote a poem for the *Worker*, urging Australians to stand by the spirit of Eureka:

---

[1] Francis Adams, quoted by Ian Turner, *The Australian Dream* (Melbourne, 1968), p. 181

So we must fly a rebel flag
As others did before us;
And we must sing a rebel song
And join in rebel chorus.
We'll make the tyrants feel the sting
Of those that they would throttle.
They needn't say the fault is ours
If blood should stain the wattle! [2]

As Rosa's father said, Eureka has become more than history. It has become a legend. And legends, like poetry, can be read in many different ways. But at the very least, the Eureka story is against bullying and tyranny. It is about the right to fight for freedom.

[2] Henry Lawson, 'Freedom on the Wallaby', *A Campfire Yarn: Henry Lawson Complete Works 1885-1900*, (Sydney, 1988), p. 146

NADIA WHEATLEY

Nadia Wheatley began writing fiction in 1976, after completing postgraduate work in Australian history. Her published work includes picture books, novels for younger readers, young adult novels, short stories (for adults as well as for young adults), history, biography and criticism. She has also written for television and the theatre.

Her first book, *Five Times Dizzy*, received the New South Wales Premier's Special Children's Book Award in 1983 and was Highly Commended in the Children's Book Council of Australia (CBCA) Awards. This was one of the first Australian children's books to celebrate the multicultural richness of our society.

Nadia Wheatley has since had four books named as CBCA Honour Books, in all three fiction categories. *My Place*, illustrated by Donna Rawlins, was the CBCA Book of the Year for Younger Readers in 1988. It also won the inaugural Eve Pownall Award (1988) for non-fiction, as well as children's choice awards and international award listings.

Over recent years, Nadia has enjoyed working with different illustrators, to produce picture books which are suitable for older readers as well as young children. These titles are *The Greatest Treasure of Charlemagne the King*, illustrated by Deborah Klein; *Highway*, illustrated by Andrew McLean; and *Luke's Way of Looking*, illustrated by Matt Ottley. *Highway* was an Honour Book in the 1999 CBCA awards, and has been shortlisted for the 2000 YABBA Award, and *Luke's Way of Looking* has been shortlisted for the 2000 CBCA Picture Book of the Year Award.